"Bethany Ann...hear our cries. In the dim light of early dawn he held us, not wrapped in loving arms but under the water instead."

A small bony hand grabbed and tore at the pond scum weeds, desperate to touch something, anything alive. "We are trapped, doomed for eternity in our watery graves. Free us."

Faces, hair, black eyes, fear, death, forever circling. Forever reaching and not finding. Voices, pleading, begging, "Bethany Ann...find Benjamin. Set us free."

Praise for R. H. Burkett

Won Oklahoma Writers Federation's 2015 Book of the Year;

Won Ozark Writers League 2010 Book of the Year

Won Storyteller Magazine People's Choice Award; The Clouse Literary Arts Award, and the 2022 Hightower Award

Four published books

Numerous contest wins.

Public speaker

Tarot Card Reader

Bad Moon Rising

by

R. H. Burkett

Bad Moon Rising

Cover Art by *Kim Mendoza*

The Wild Rose Press, Inc.
PO Box 708
Adams Basin, NY 14410-0708
Visit us at www.thewildrosepress.com

Publishing History
First Edition, 2023
Trade Paperback ISBN 978-1-5092-4987-9
Digital ISBN 978-1-5092-4988-6

Previously Published 2018-Pen-L Publishing
Published in the United States of America

Dedication

For all demon-fighters

"Good always destroys evil."

Bethany Ann

Chapter 1

"Sister Rachel Ellen is walking through the valley of the shadow of death. Leave her be."

These words, hissed through clenched, yellowed teeth, belonged to a woman as vile as the serpents Daddy let crawl up his arm and around his neck at prayer meeting. That was Mama she was talking about. No power in heaven or earth could keep me from slipping behind Aunt Hester's back and tiptoeing into Mama's bedroom.

That's when I saw them. Gathered around her bed. Angels, standing together—waiting. At the window one stood taller than the hundred-year-old Cypress tree down at the swamp. Snow-white wings caught sunlight streaming through the glass and threw shimmering rays across the room brighter than pearls on frosted ice. She would be the one to take Mama by the hand and lead her across.

I studied Mama looking for Death. I didn't find him hiding in the wrinkles and grooves that etched her small face. Mama never got sick. Aunt Hester lied. No doubt to torment me. The bitch.

Mama looked like always. Well, maybe there was a hint of paleness around her mouth and a funny rattle to her breathing but certainly not anything close to the feared shadow of Death. Then again, what was Death supposed to look like, anyway?

"Is that you, Bethany Ann?"

"Yes, Mama," I said and took her outstretched hand in mine.

Her hands looked the same too. Hard and calloused from years of scrubbing clothes on the old washboard out back and permanently faded from the harsh lye soap. Washing, cooking, and cleaning, that was Mama in a nutshell. Probably would be the exact words chiseled on her tombstone too. Of course those words would be below *Rachel Wayne, devoted wife of Reverend Jedidiah Wayne.*

Daddy always took top billing.

"Child, I'll not make it through this night and they be things you need to know. You hear me out now. No back-talking. Understand?"

"Yes, em'." The spit in my mouth dried to sand.

"I put up with your brothers only because I birthed them and a mother's duty is to her young'uns. But I don't like them. They are their daddy's sons. Arrogant, lustful, deceitful, lying hypocrites the whole lot of 'em."

I'd never heard her talk this way before. Truth be known, Mama didn't talk much at all since Daddy's opinion was the only one what mattered. Her deep backwoods Louisiana accent came thick as bees on a honeycomb. Clipped words, bitter as dandelion greens poured from her mouth. Perhaps Death was here after all, wringing the truth out of her frail little body.

"Oh, how I despised being forced to marry a snake-handling, talking-in tongues- preacher man. Detested being barefoot, pregnant, and in the kitchen. Always cooking, cleaning, and scrubbing the floor only to have his slimy, smelly serpents crawl across it. Every night fearing that stinking big copper rattler of his would curl

2

beside me in my own bed. And oh, how I loathe Jedidiah Wayne."

She gave my hand a small squeeze. "But I love you, Bethany Ann, more than life itself, and I thank God your blood has not one drop of Wayne it in." She gazed up at heaven. "Praise be to God you are not from that holier-than-thou Jedidiah Wayne's loins."

I threw a quick glance at Snow Angel expecting to see a bolt of lightning streak across the sky for Mama's blasphemy. None came. What was Mama saying? Must be seeing things. That's what it was. She was out of her head. I searched her face for signs of fever, but her eyes stared back at me crystal clear. A smug smile pulled at her dry, colorless lips like she was about to reveal a deep, dark secret. A secret she'd held captive all these years and at last would set free.

"You heard me right, child. Jedidiah Wayne is not your father."

It wasn't shock that brought the sting of tears to my eyes. It was relief.

I hated the ground Daddy walked on and vowed one day to kill him.

Chapter 2

"Hush now and listen to what I tell you," Mama demanded.

Her voice softened and the sharp edges and lines around her eyes and mouth smoothed like rich cream.

"Your real daddy came to me one hot, sultry July night. Took my hand and led me into the bayou where the wind blew cool off the water, and the smell of honeysuckle and magnolia hung heavy like a line of wet sheets in the air. Sinfully handsome he was with hair dark as coal and skin the color of burnt copper.

"I remember the feel of my sweaty hand in his firm grip. His intoxicating scent of wind and rain. I told him he was no God-fearing Christian man to tempt me so. He threw back his head and laughed, deep and rich and said, 'I bow to no man, and kneel only before the altar of The Church of the Howling Moon.'

Memories had a hold of Mama now, and I felt her being pulled from me. She continued on. The Angels continued to wait.

"I laughed back at him and said, "Never heard of any such foolishness. Weren't no church called that and there be no such thing as a howling moon.

"And there in that swamp surrounded by cypress trees draped in yards of lacy Spanish moss and full of the sounds of the night, he pointed to the inky sky. The moon hung full and round like a burnt-orange fireball ready to bust apart at the seams.

" '*That* be a howling moon,' he said. 'A moon so beautiful that one look turns your blood to a river of black fire racing through your veins. A moon so powerful it can drive you insane unless you yield to its pull and run and howl into the wild.'

"We walked hand-in-hand along the water's edge and when he pulled me down onto the damp moss-covered ground, I melted into him. I gazed up at his eyes, darker than midnight and watched the crescent moon rise in them.

" 'I think you be more spirit than man,' " I whispered to him.

"I should've been scared but it weren't fear that made my body weak. Desire, like none I'd ever imagined possible washed over me. His touch was gentle and kind. His kisses, cool sweetness against my fevered skin. The love we made mixed with the raw and wild of the bayou. I gripped his arms to keep from falling into pure rapture."

She took a ragged gulp of air.

I bit my lip.

"I'd resigned myself to a life of harsh, often violent days with Jedidiah, void of all joy. I never regretted doing what I did that night. The happiness that consumed me for that brief hour deep in the untamed Louisiana wetlands was worth a lifetime of hell."

Never had I seen Mama smile the way she did then. It made me happy and sad all at the same time. It was a few minutes before she spoke again.

"Then as quick and mysterious as he came, he was gone. I woke up next to Jedidiah. Heartbroken, I turned my head to the wall and cried silent tears. It had only been a dream. A vision born out of a desperate need to be loved, cherished, like every woman yearns to be. Nine months later when they laid you in my arms, and I saw the same crescent moon in your violet eyes, I knew."

Goose bumps popped along my arm. Mama squeezed my hand again and sighed deep.

"I knew I'd given birth to a daughter of the Howling Moon."

Chapter 3

"That's why I'm different, ain't it Mama? Why I don't hold with Jedidiah's beliefs."

"Yes, child." Mama's voice weakened and she motioned to me. "Come closer."

I crawled beside her and laid my head on her shoulder. The coldness of her body next to my heat made me shiver and caused a memory of my own to take me by the hand and lead me away.

A recollection of one very rare bone chillin' day when I took a shortcut walking home from school and cut through Granny LeBeaux's back forty, washed over me, a memory I'd tucked way back into the dark corners of my mind.

I didn't have a pair of mittens to my name and wore a pair of Mama's cotton socks on my hands instead. The cardboard in my boots covered the holes but didn't stop the cold from sneakin' in. The fact that I thought spooky, toothless ol' lady LeBeaux was a *Voodooienne* and probably had shrunken heads and dead chickens hanging in every window, didn't matter much that day. My fingers turning into popsicles did.

Mama pulled me tight to her side and Granny LeBeaux's face crawled back into the shadows. Many nights when I was a child, Mama would hold me this way before I drifted off to sleep. She'd whisper stories in my ear about far-away places and make-believe worlds.

Even at that young age, I knew she risked a surefire come-to-Jesus beating for telling me those pagan fairy tales. Of course, to my way of thinking, Cinderella walking around in glass slippers weren't any more far-fetched than a man walking on water. However, there was no book in the Bible called Cinderella, so the fairy tales were our little secret. Just like me seeing angels and knowing things before they happened.

"Jedidiah noticed right off you were turned different from the boys but figured it was because you be female. I never feared him finding out you weren't his. I have his arrogance to thank for that. He'd never dream any man would have the nerve to fool with his woman. Or more to the point, his woman ever lusting after another man after laying with him."

"He's crazy, isn't he, Mama? He thinks he's Jesus."

"Crazy? Yes. Jesus? No." A small snort. "He thinks he's God."

She pulled me closer to her side. Took all the strength she had, but when I protested she hushed me with one of her *don't-fool-with-me-child* looks.

"Jedidiah is a wicked man, Bethany Ann. Sick and twisted. He lusts after young girls."

This should've sent me wheeling. It didn't. And was the main reason why I hated him so. But for Mama to voice the dirty little secret made supper rumble in my belly and parade up my throat. I swallowed hard.

"I turned a blind eye to his evilness," Mama confessed. "And for that, I will no doubt burn in hell. I'd watch in dread and fear when he searched the congregation, hunting, stalking the one he wanted. He's particularly fond of small, blonde, green-eyed—

"Mama, please. I don't want—

"You must!"

Her outburst caused cornbread and beans to take up their march again. I gazed at the angels and silently prayed to them to keep me from throwing up all over Grandma Polly's patchwork quilt.

"You must."

Mama's tone lost its sting.

"He'd start out slow. Just a harmless touching of their hair and singing praises to Jesus for their innocence and beauty. Their folks would beam with pride when the glorious Jedidiah Wayne pointed out their daughters as examples of God's beautiful work and holy righteousness. And when he pulled them into the baptismal to anoint them with the power of the Holy Spirit, no one followed or protested. None thought it wrong. But I knew better."

She spit those last words hard as nails.

I shuddered and moved away from her.

"He'd rape the innocence and beauty right out of those young'uns. In the name of Jesus Christ. Violated. Molested. Swear them to secrecy with threats of hellfire and eternal damnation if they told. To this day, none ever have."

Sickness overtook me and my stomach lurched. That wasn't true. One had. Sarah Rose.

My best friend.

Chapter 4

Sarah Rose lived a whoop and holler from our back porch if you cut through the swamp otherwise she lived about four miles down the road. We were in the same grade at school and were just naturally drawn to each other like a moth to flame.

Folks said we could've been sisters, but I don't know why. Sarah Rose and me were different as night and day. Standing by her side, my hair shone like India Ink and my skin glowed like dark rich honey next to her wheat-spun hair and peaches-and-cream complexion. While my eyes were deep violet, hers were green as gooseberries. I moved with cat-like grace and she was always tripping over something. She blamed her clumsiness on her sister's hand-me-down shoes that were too big for her tiny feet.

Sarah Rose was no bigger than a chigger in the grass.

We shared everything.

I told her about my visions.

She told me about the night Daddy violated her.

Good Christian folks from miles around traveled days to attend one of Reverend Jedidiah's famous revivals. He could summon the Holy Ghost and whip a congregation into a lathered frenzy with his fire and brimstone voice and hissing serpents. That night he'd outdone himself and had literally preached up a storm.

All day long the air hung stagnant and stale. Tree branches drooped to the ground. Even the flies swarmed and droned in lazy circles as if they be weights tied to their wings. Clouds looked like heavy dumplings stewing in puke green gravy. I felt jittery and out of sorts.

Something bad was fixin' to happen.

Thunder grumbled in the distance. The wood-framed church, packed to the gills, spilled over and oozed madness bordering on mass hysteria. Outside lightning zigzagged to the ground, while inside the charged air fairly crackled and popped. The church simmered like a pressure cooker on low just itchin' to blow its lid. One spark and the whole place would've gone up in a blaze of glory. Folks fell down in the aisles, jerking and convulsing, speaking all manner of garbled nonsense.

Oh-So-Proper Aunt Hester tore at the pins that held her mousey gray locks in a skin-stretching knot at the back of her head and ripped them from her hair. Her head flung from side to side like a foaming dog. Possessed and supposedly full of the Holy Spirit, she thrashed about like a wild jungle monkey in heat.

The storm grew in strength and so did Jedidiah's yelling and hollering. Sweat ran in rivulets down his neck and stained the armpits of his starched white shirt. The stink of men's unwashed bodies and sweetly-perfumed women crawled across the floor on all fours. Folks fanned themselves with any stiff paper they could find. I struggled for a deep breath.

Jedidiah kept pace with the thunder and lightning. His Bible took a beatin' and his voice boomed.

"Praise Jesus! Hallelujah!"

Everyone had lost their ever-loving minds.

Big green eyes nearly popped from Sarah Rose's head when Jedidiah pointed his finger at her and yelled, "Praise Jesus for this cherished lamb of God! Glory be to Heaven!"

Every eye trained on her and shouts of "Amen, Brother Jed, amen!" shook the walls.

Sarah Rose trembled like a scared rabbit searching for a hole to hide in.

Jedidiah's dark eyes glowed like glazed onyx and fixed on Sarah's chest that rose and fell rapid and exaggerated from each terrified breath. So very much like the vipers he adored, he slithered to her side and touched her yellow hair. Soft and gentle, he'd weave the silky curls between his thin fingers. Every now and again his tongue would flick over dry lips.

My skin crawled. His touching made me want to run to the creek to scrub myself clean. It felt wrong, wasn't right. I couldn't put my finger on it, but it was creepy and made me squirm.

Sarah Rose didn't know straight up from sic'em. She looked at her ma and pa silently pleading for them to reach out for her. Madness had them in its grasp and they ignored her. Eyes wide and panic-stricken, her gaze darted around the room till she locked on mine. I heard her desperate screams for help in my head. I leaped up only to have Mama jerk me back down onto the hard pew.

I shot a quick glance at Mama. She went pale as milk toast when Jedidiah led Sarah away into the baptism room. "To pray for her immortal soul."

I didn't see Sarah Rose at school for a week after that night. "Feelin' puny" was the only explanation I got. When I finally met up with her, she'd changed. I couldn't explain it but somehow she was different, inside and out. She'd shuffle along, dragging her small bare feet in the dirt and never look me in the eye. In fact, she didn't focus on anyone or anything. Usually, she'd jabber like a magpie over nothing, but I could barely get a "hey" out of her. Then one day, out of the blue, she said, "I want to go to Grandpa's."

The swamp was home. I craved its wildness. Its danger. Beauty and mystery. I went there every chance I got, skipping along the moss-covered trails and paths memorizing every twist and turn, every tree and bush. My favorite spot was underneath a giant cypress tree I nick-named Grandpa. Sarah Rose hated the very things I loved about the swamp, so when she suggested we go there, a creepy-crawling feeling stirred in my belly.

We hadn't sat beneath Grandpa Cypress five minutes before she broke into gut-wrenching sobs that scared the starch plumb out of me.

"What?"

"Your daddy ruined me."

I gagged when she described how Jedidiah kissed her so hard, her lips bruised. Gasped when she showed me the blackish-blue and yellow marks where he'd pawed and fondled. Threw my guts up when she said he'd damned near split her in half.

I reached for her and crushed her to my chest. Our tears joined together. But where she wept from shame, guilt, humiliation, and pain, I cried tears of raw-meat-red fury.

"You told your mama, didn't you? What did she say?"

This question threw her into another fit of tears. "Told me I was thirteen and old enough to be with a man and how honored I should be that the blessed Reverend Jedidiah Wayne picked me to make a woman out of."

"Are you shittin' me?"

My swearing always drew a smile from her which was usually the reason why I did it. But this time, shock pushed the curse from my mouth. I wanted to yank out every hair from her mama's head. What a vile, disgusting thing to say.

"You ought not cuss, Bethany Ann. If your ma heard ya, she'd wash your mouth out with lye soap, or worse."

"Probably." I laughed then winked. "But she ain't never gonna catch me."

She stared at me then with those big frog-green eyes of hers and said in a little voice, "Why, didn't you see it? You see other things. I'm your best friend, and you did nothing. Why didn't you stop him?"

My insides shriveled and curled like a piece of fatback sizzling in a cast iron skillet. Her blaming hit me hard.

"I tried to run to ya. Mama wouldn't let me. I've told you a hundred times I don't have any control over what or when I see things. You got to believe I would've found a way to stop him if I'd knowed."

"I know."

Yeah, we both knew. But that didn't stop guilt from taking a bite out of my butt.

"Sarah Rose, I promise. I won't let him get you again."

I kept a tight watch over Sarah Rose. Every time Jedidiah headed her way, I'd run between them and steer her off in another direction. I'd stand beside her at meeting and hold her hand. Usually I sat with Mama but when I told her, "I need to be next to Sarah Rose," she nodded her head and whispered, "That's a fine idea, child."

I couldn't protect them all, but I made damn sure Jedidiah never laid a hand on Sarah Rose after that day.

Two years passed before we talked about what had happened again. Sarah Rose, a few days short of turning fifteen, was moving away. When her daddy ran off with "that red-headed harlot from the Winn Dixie," her Mama decided to move to Natchez, Mississippi to live with her sister's family. Sarah Rose and me said teary goodbyes in our secret place, under Grandpa Cypress. I gave her a special gift I'd made just for her.

"What's this funny ol' thing tied to this strip of leather?" she asked.

"A bobcat claw. Seen it last week when I was walking along the creek. Bobcat medicine is powerful and fierce. No one will mess with you as long as you wear it. Them bobcats are mean son-of-a-bitches, ya know."

"You ever gonna stop your swearing?"

"Probably not."

She laughed and hugged the crude necklace to her heart. "You're turning into a regular witchy woman of the night, what with finding claws and making protection spells. Best be careful. Jedidiah ever catch you, he'd strip you naked and beat the sap out of you, shouting hallelujah with every lick of the strap and rock hard between the legs."

"Probably." I laughed then winked. "But he ain't never gonna catch me."

"I gotta git. Ma's waiting."

In my heart I knew I'd never see my friend again. I yelled out, "Sarah Rose?"

My shout stopped her cold, and she turned to face me.

"I promise. Someday. Somehow. I'll kill him for what he did to you and the others. I swear it."

She walked back to me, surefooted and straight, and gazed deep into my eyes. An unspoken bond of sisterhood passed between us that I couldn't put into words but felt the tug just the same. She shivered.

"You scare me, Bethany Ann. From that dark, spooky look in your eyes, I have no doubt that you will," she whispered. "But they'll do worse than beat you if you're caught. They'll toss you in jail and throw away the key. Maybe even hang you."

"Probably." I laughed then winked. "But they ain't never gonna catch me."

Chapter 5

Mama's gulp for air shook me free from the memories of Sarah Rose. Mama's color had turned to wheat paste. Snow Angel moved from the window and stood at the foot of the bed.

It wouldn't be long now.

"I left you some things," Mama panted. "Put them in a bag under your bed. There isn't much. Your grandma's tortoiseshell brush and comb set and a gold locket are the only things I have of value. But I wanted you to have them. Knowing that dried-up prune of a sister-in-law of mine, if I didn't give them to you before I died, you'd never see them after. There be a few more things you'll need as well."

I winced at the mention of Aunt Hester. She and I hated one another from the get go. I could see straight through her holier-than-thou act right into her black heart and she knew it.

"Bethany Ann? I want you to promise me something."

"Yes 'em?"

"Jedidiah not only has lust in his heart for the girls at meeting, but has a powerful hunger for you as well. When you turned thirteen and started to fill out, I saw the fever in his eyes. True, he favors the fair, light-skinned girls more, but for some reason he's drawn to your darkness.

"I flat out told him if he ever touched a hair on your head, I'd come to him in the deep sleep of night, slit his throat from ear-to-ear and laugh while he choked and gurgled on his own blood. I'd hack him into little pieces, toss the meat to the swamp gators and swear to everyone he'd just disappeared, maybe even ascended."

Her chuckle came dry and low without humor and edged with frosted wickedness.

"That was the day *I* put the fear of God into Jedidiah Wayne."

Shocked, I scooted back on the bed till my back bumped the wall behind me. It took a few seconds for me to realize my mouth hung open. This dying woman was no Mama I'd ever knowed.

I loved Mama but always wondered why she let Daddy tromp on her like dirt. I figured it was because he was too strong and had worn her out. He'd slapped her down too many times and like the red-roan horse he prized, her will and spirit had splintered into tiny pieces.

This fire and ice was a new side to her and it made me proud. Tears nipped at my eyelids. It wasn't fair. Just when I was learning there was more strength to Mama than what met the eye, Death waited to jerk her away from me. I would never know her dreams. Her thoughts. I'd been cheated out of my chance to know Mama like a best friend.

"For three years that warning held him off. But I won't be cold in my grave before he comes for you."

A shiver ran up my spine.

"Run away from here, child and don't you never look back."

"Run? Where?" My voice trembled.

"Oh, Bethany Ann, you know where. The woods.

The swamp. The Wilds has pulled you to them ever since you was big enough to walk. It's only fittin'. It was where you were conceived, and your daddy's spirit runs hot in your veins. The crescent moon be in your eyes, girl. Always remember, you're a daughter of the Howling Moon and bow before no man. Don't wait till they put me in my grave, girl. Go tonight. Promise me."

"I promise, Mama."

Weary and spent, she flopped back against the pillows and her breath came shallow. "Are they here, child?"

"Yes. They have been all along."

"Angels or demons?"

"Angels, Mama."

"Well, I have you to thank for that. You are my salvation. My pride and joy. The only good thing what ever happened to me." She turned her head, stared me straight in the eye, and gave my hand a small squeeze. "I love you, my beautiful Bethany Ann."

For a few moments everything stood still. The only sound in the room was Grandma's cuckoo clock ticking off the minutes. Then the flutter of wings stirred the air and radiant light covered the room like creamy smooth liquid sunshine. Every frazzled nerve in me quieted. Grief dissolved like sugar in water. Pure joy flooded and filled me to the brim. Just as I knowed, Snow Angel reached for Mama's hand. Together they passed through the window pane and floated upward airy and light like cotton candy wisps in the wind.

I glanced back at the bed. How small and worn-out Mama's shell of a body looked sunk deep into blankets and pillows. I had just witnessed the greatest wonder on earth. I'd seen firsthand the splendor and glory of The

Crossing, of life after death. Even still, I couldn't hold back the tears streaming down my face.

But I didn't weep for Mama's death.

I wept for her life. Or lack of one.

If only the grit and gumption she showed while dying had been there in life, maybe her days would've been worth living. If only she never set eyes on Jedidiah Wayne. If only—

The hair on the back of my arm pricked. Hester was on her way.

I scurried down the hall to my room.

It would be hours before anyone bothered to knock on my door to tell me Mama was gone.

Chapter 6

The stink of Dapper Dan hair jelly mixed with dried sweat covered me before Jedidiah did.

Why hadn't I run? I'd meant to. But sleep overtook me.

Earlier, I sat in the middle of the hardwood floor, pulled Mama's bag out from underneath the bed and searched its contents. There wasn't any money, but the things she'd stuffed into that tattered cloth-covered satchel were priceless. Three pairs of my brother's overalls and work shirts were worth their weight in gold.

I hated the long, buttoned-to-the-collar Puritan dresses I was made to endure. It was a sin to wear men's trousers, said so someplace in the Good Book, which, of course, was written by men. How convenient. I think Jedidiah feared pants would somehow change a woman into thinking like a man. Like that was anything to brag about.

Mama had snorted and said the reason had nothin' to do with God. It was easier and quicker to hike up a woman's skirt, bend her over, and get a piece than wasting time unbuttoning trousers. What that meant, I didn't exactly know but the bitterness in her voice told me not to ask.

The black tennis shoes made me gasp.

I'd seen the running shoes at Baker's Emporium downtown. The sign in the window claimed you could run farther and jump higher with them and since my most favorite thing to do in the whole world was run, I ached to try them out.

I knew better than to ask for a pair. Jedidiah would've smacked me a good one for even thinking about wanting such sinful things. How Mama got the money and managed to slip away and buy them, I'd never know now, but the sting of tears burned when I tied the dingy-white shoelaces into a tight bow. It didn't matter that they were slightly used with tiny holes around the toes. To my mind, those canvas shoes were as grand as Cinderella's glass slippers.

The drab granny dress hit the floor, and I slipped into the overalls easy and smooth like a hand into a leather glove. I stuffed the dress and my scarred lace-up boots into the carpetbag. I might need them.

Thoughts to hurry and run nagged at me but weariness pushed heavy on top of my head. Surely to God, Jedidiah wouldn't try anything so soon. I'd catch a few hours of sleep then sneak off under cover of deep night.

What a huge mistake. But for Jedidiah. Not me.

"No!"

Like a wild cat, I fought him. Kicking, screaming, biting. My thrashing about was like kerosene to flame. A nasty, twisted grin spread across his face.

"I knew you'd be worth the wait," he hissed into my ear. "Your mama just lay there, like a used-up old tow sack. But I knew that dark smoke in your eyes meant there be fire between your legs. Three long years I waited for this day."

Raspy, rough, and smelly his slimy tongue licked up the side of my face like a cow slurping a saltlick. "We got all night and the rest of your life to make up for lost time." His rancid breath burned like fire on my neck.

The rest of my life? Panic shot through me. Small fists hammered against his broad chest. I screamed.

He laughed.

"She-devil," he spat. "Holler all ya want, nobody will hear, and I like it."

Warm spit hit my face and inched down my cheek. The sour taste of vomit crawled up the back of my throat.

He cackled like a lunatic. High-pitched and feral. My breath flew out in one whoosh when he dropped his knee across my chest. Dark eyes, fevered and frenzied, glowed above me like the prophesied Beast of Revelation. One huge hand pinned both of mine behind my head while the other shot between my legs and pried them apart.

"Please Daddy, don't," I whimpered.

He stared right through me and rubbed his hardness against the denim grunting like a filthy, slobbering boar hog. Long fingers tore at the buttons on my overalls.

"Sinner!" he swore, reared back and backhanded me hard across the face. Stars exploded in my head, and I tasted bitter blood oozing from a split lip.

His voice shook with fury and matched the crazed look in his eyes. "The woman shall not wear that which pertaineth unto a man, for all that do so are an abomination unto the Lord thy God. Deuteronomy 22:5."

Jedidiah Wayne was loonier than a bed bug.

When the strong material didn't give way, he crushed his lips into mine, kissing me hard.

His tongue pushed against my clenched teeth. Tears streamed down my cheeks, mixed with the snot and blood and trickled into my mouth, choking me. Each gasp for air, an icepick jabbed my side. My head throbbed. Strength ran away with hope leaving me spent and desperate.

There was no place to run. No one to hear my screams. My heart jumped and slammed against my ribs over and over like a trapped grasshopper hits the lid of fruit jar fighting against all odds for one more breath, one more chance for escape—for life.

The room spun. Everything blurred. Blackness started to edge the corners of my mind. There was only one thing I could think of to stop Jedidiah from tearing me apart, from killing me.

I cried out to the angels.

Deep.

Deep.

Deep.

Deep down, buried in the roots of my very soul, a mighty strength began to surge.

A feelin' of power so strong, fear knelt before it, flooded my whole body and mind.

This rape…this violation…would…not…happen.

He wanted a struggle? A fight? Oh, preacher-man, be careful what you wish for.

Eyes squeezed tight, I settled deep into myself and called forth the energy and strength stored in every thought, bone, muscle, and sinew. I let his tongue in. Then bit down.

He jumped back like a scalded dog, freeing me.

I rolled off the side of the bed and flattened myself against the wall. Streams of sweaty, black hair fell about my face and shoulders. Blood from a busted lip stained the front of my shirt. Fingernails dug into wood, leaving scratch marks running up the wall, as flat palms curled into fists. Like a cornered animal, a low snarl rose from my throat. Eyes narrow, I willed him closer.

" 'Vengeance is mine, saith the Lord.' Romans 12:19" Was that really my voice, deadly cool and granite hard that taunted him?

Shock flew across his face and a wicked chuckle spewed forth from someplace way down in my gut.

"Witch!" he screamed and lunged for me.

That's when it happened.

A tiny whispering came to my ears. "The crescent moon be in your eyes, girl. You bow before no man."

Time stopped.

A jungle cat slinked around the room on paws silent as death. Black as sin, shining eyes of hazel ice, the jaguar hugged the floor and circled, tense and stealthy. She crouched low, ready to pounce. A deep growl vibrated the walls and wood floor.

A quick swipe of claws.

Flesh peeled from Jedidiah's right ear, across his eyes and lips and down his left side.

I felt tender skin give way. Smelled his fear. Tasted the blood.

He let out a howl that would make every one of Uncle Ezekiel's prized coon dogs jealous. Trembling hands flew to his face. Blood spilled over thin, long fingers and colored the floor crimson.

Lightning fast, I streaked out the back door, leapt the garden gate without breaking stride, easy as stepping over a log.

I ran.

Ran like I had raven wings on my feet instead of tennis shoes.

Ran like I'd never tire or need a deep breath ever

again.

Ran like I could run forever.

The night surrounded me, dark as pitch, but I didn't need light. I knew the way to the swamp like the back of my hand. Even if I didn't, it wouldn't have mattered. My eyes captured everything sharp and crystal clear.

Grandpa Cypress waited for me with open arms. In three bounds, my feet hardly touched his hide as I climbed to a high limb. Settled on the thick branch, ears pricked, I listened to the night. Far away I picked up the sounds of yelling and swearing. No doubt Jedidiah had my half-wit brothers looking for me. For sure he'd promised them a piece of the prize if they found me.

Well, let them come.

I'd crush their skulls between sharp teeth and strong jaws.

For the jaguar and me were one.

Chapter 7

"Ben, I hate askin' this of you, son, but I gotta send ya into the swamps. I don't believe for one minute there's a jaguar running loose, but there's a girl missin' and it's our duty to investigate."

Benjamin Sol shrugged his large shoulders and grinned. Leaned back in his tattered office chair, boots propped up on the desk, hands laced behind his head, Buford Tate was the perfect picture of a backwoods parish sheriff.

"I don't mind, boss."

"Even still, it's a hell of a thing to ask of a newly-hired deputy, but I'm too old, too tired, and too fat to go traipsing around some mosquito-infested swamp on a wild goose chase. Besides, to be honest, there's things that goes on in there that scares the bejesus out of me."

"Guess that means you believe the story Wayne's telling about some Voodoo priest conjuring up an evil panther to kill him, steal his daughter, and turn her into some kind of zombie?"

The chair groaned in protest when the sheriff leaned forward and smacked the desk with the flat of his hand. "I don't believe one GD word of it. This here is French Loosianna. Voodoo carrying on is as common as red beans and rice. I've been sheriff here nigh on twenty year, and I ain't had no trouble with them folks. Wayne's been Bible-beatin' almost as long. Why all of a sudden would they be after him?"

"He claims it's because he's spreading the word of God, and they don't like it."

"Bullshit."

Another smile spread across Ben's square face. Buford didn't mince words. He liked that about the man. "Have you ever met Jedidiah Wayne?"

"Once. Ben? Why you always have to pace the room like a caged circus animal? Plant that skinny butt of yours in a chair, son."

Ben laughed. "Sorry. I think better on the move."

Before sitting, he pulled the shade on the front window to block out the early afternoon sun. The mercury thermometer with the picture of Speedy Alka-Seltzer hanging next to the door, registered a cool 85. The wood and wicker ceiling fan whirled and groaned above him. He twirled a straight-back chair around and sat on it backward. "You were saying?"

"The wife dragged me to one of Wayne's revivals a few years back. To hear her talk, he was the second coming of Christ. That was one of the wildest nights of my life. Heard tell those Catholics are pros at hittin' the rail, but they ain't got nothing on them holy rollers. Folks were droppin' to the floor like flies, squirming, and wiggling around like a can of worms, jabbering all sorts of strange gobbledygook.

"Outside, thunder boomed and lightning lit up the sky. Inside, Wayne had those damn snakes of his revved up, hissin' and spittin'—

"Snakes?"

"Yep. Rattlers. Copperheads. Moccasins. He's got a real love affair goin' on with those critters. Tells you a lot about the man right there, don't it? Gotta' be a dang fool to play with things that can kill with one bite."

"A dang fool or a madman," Sol said.

"My point exactly."

Buford rummaged in his desk for a pack of Juicy Fruit. He crammed a stick in his mouth and chewed hard. "That in itself didn't make me too fond of the feller." Snap. Pop. Snap. Pop. "But what tipped the scales heavy was when he went after the Walker girl. He took her to the back room to pray special for her."

Ben's stomach cramped. Crimes against the innocent and helpless sickened him and was the main reason he pinned on a star. Painful memories, ones he'd stuffed deep down inside, started to churn. "You think he hurt the girl?"

Snap. Pop. Snap. Pop. "Not that I can prove. Sarah Rose Walker was cuter than a little bug's ear. Big green eyes. Hair yeller as ripe corn. Quick mind. Always askin' questions. Could talk a blue streak. She was never the same after that night."

Ben ran his fingers through his short, dark hair. "You think he did more in that backroom than a laying-on-of-hands?"

"Oh, I'd bet the farm he laid-on-hands alright, just not in a religious-saving-of-the-soul kind of way. But Jess Walker never said a word. And you know, same as me, we can't go bustin' down doors without no good reason."

"You think Wayne harmed his daughter in some way and is covering it up with this Voodoo story of his?"

"Can't say for sure, maybe just my sheriff gut working overtime. But, one thing's for dang certain. Something tore the hell out of that preacher-man. Doc said his ear was damn near ripped off. Took almost a yard of catgut to sew him up. Doubt a human could do that."

Ben pulled his .357 from its holster and checked the cylinder. "Ok, Boss. I'll head for the swamp and take a look see."

Buford cleared his throat. "Ah, Ben? Before ya go, I got one more thing I gotta ask of you."

"Sure thing. Name it."

"I want you to go see a fortune teller."

Chapter 8

The cardboard sign in the window read: *Lady Tibatha: Tarot Reader*

Ben stood on the front steps of the little shop and shook his head. Crazy. He was crazy to agree to this. He didn't believe in fortune tellers, destiny, the supernatural, or even some supreme being for that matter. How many times had he begged God to heal Mom? One hundred? Two hundred? His prayers fell on deaf ears. Mom died anyway.

The fire in his belly flared. Absent-mindedly, he rubbed at the pain, a grimace twisted his tanned face.

Then war broke out. If God Is Love, why did He allow man's inhumanity to man? The memory of exploding shells, rifle fire, and men screaming in agony haunted his dreams too many times to believe in a power greater than himself. No, God didn't exist. People's fate was of their own making.

To hell with this. Even if she did have her finger on the pulse of the bayou like Buford had claimed, he still had no use for fortune telling. He turned to go.

An orange cat strolled around the side of the house and pranced up the steps. Tail high, he head-butted the front door, looked at Ben, and gave a scratchy meow. Oh hell. It was too hot to be outside for long. He'd just open the door a crack and let the tomcat in. A tinkling bell betrayed his presence. A butter-smooth voice, flavored with a thick Jamaican accent, came from behind the counter.

"Welcome, Benjamin Sol. I be waiting for you."

Buford, you ol' son-of-a-bitch. He should've known the crafty sheriff would've called ahead and given Lady Tibatha a heads-up.

Ben stepped in and gave the shop a quick look-see. Lucky charms. Love potions. Tarot cards. Books on Wiccan, Voodoo, and Religions of the World. Curious stuff, but the main thing that struck him was how cool and shaded the room was—and the wonderful smell.

Sweet, pleasant, yet strange and exotic, the scent of jasmine, sandalwood, patchouli and other unidentifiable perfumes and incense leaked from every nook and cranny. One odor dominated the rest. He knew that aroma. What was it? He searched his mind, knowing the answer lurked somewhere in memory, but he'd kept the gate on the past locked so long it'd rusted shut and he couldn't put his finger on what he needed.

Lady Tibatha glided across the room on bare feet silent as cat paws. The skirts on her leopard-print caftan made small swish-swish sounds with every step. She flipped the Open sign to Closed and locked the door. Ben cocked an eyebrow.

"You come."

What the hell had he walked into? He followed her through a beaded curtain into of all places, the kitchen. Bright yellow cupboards lined one wall. Crystals hung in the windows and cast small rainbows across the wood floor. Again, he noticed the coolness, but it didn't come from the black metal fan that hummed on the kitchen counter.

He couldn't explain the feeling that washed over

him but it reminded him of childhood. Of warm summer nights after a day of play when he and his sister, Danni lay exhausted underneath the giant oak tree in the backyard. The refreshing feel of a light, cool breeze brushing against skin that melted the sting of the day's heat into nothing.

Those were happy times. Why did this cozy kitchen make him feel that way? How could a room give comfort like an old shade tree?

Tibatha pointed to the simple wooden kitchen table and chairs. "Sit."

Ben twirled the chair around and sat on it backwards. Orange cat leapt onto the table and rubbed against his hand.

"Dat be Sylvester." Tibatha's hands waved back and forth when she talked. "Him think he lion. I tell him no different. It good to believe in something." Her head cocked to the side and she gave a Cheshire cat grin. "Is dat not true? Benjamin Sol?"

He squirmed.

Not wanting an answer, she turned, opened the icebox, and poured whiskey-colored liquid into a jelly jar. She handed the glass to him. He took a small sip. Sassafras! That was the mystery scent in the room. A grin spread from ear-to-ear.

"I haven't had cold sassafras tea in years." He smacked his lips. "Mom used to give it to me when . . ." More thoughts of Mom strangled his words. Why were memories of her bubbling to the top after so many years of pushing them down?

Tibatha pulled out a chair and eased her willowy frame onto it. "When your stomach hurt." She finished his sentence. "You drink now. Will ease the fire in your belly. But the pain in your heart? Not so much."

Over the glass rim, he stared at the woman sitting across of him. She unnerved him. How did she know his stomach ached on and off for years? Or the secrets he carried? And she didn't look like anything he had pictured, either. Weren't fortune tellers supposed to be older than dirt, wrinkled as prunes, wild-eyed, and witchy-haired?

Lady Tibatha or Tibby as Buford called her, was none of these things. Tall and graceful as a dancer she moved like liquid silk. Hair the color of smoke fell straight around a heart-shaped face of creamy, dark chocolate. No crow's feet tracked the corners of her eyes. In fact, the only lines that marked her face where the ones years of laughter etched around her ruby-red lipsticked mouth. He'd be hard-pressed to venture an age, but he guessed late fifty's, early sixties. Eyes, dark and shiny as ebony, studied him back. Understanding, compassionate eyes so deep he could fall into them and never crawl out. Lady Tibatha was beautiful. Twenty years ago, she would've been striking.

He could well imagine the shock on deputy Buford Tate's face when Lady Tibatha had first walked into the St. Clair Parish Sheriff's Office, twenty years back. An escaped murderer from Cummins State Farm in Arkansas had run to the swamps of Louisiana to hide out. A full-blown manhunt complete with the best bloodhounds in the parish had turned up nothing. Lady Tibatha claimed she knew where the convict was hiding from a dream she had. No one believed her. No one. Except Buford Tate.

Quite a feather in his cap when he brought the felon in, single-handed. Got him elected sheriff the next year and every year since then. The folks of St. Clair Parish never forget and were nothing if not loyal. Twenty years and fifty pounds ago, Buford Tate would've cut a handsome figure. Maybe he and Tibby's relationship was more than a professional one, no matter how taboo.

"She's just another colored son." Stepfather's raspy voice rang in his ears.

"Why you come to Lady Tibatha?"

Her question jarred him into the present and, thankfully, dissolved stepfather's voice into the nails and boards of the small house.

"Didn't Sheriff Tate explain it to you?" A blank stare. "When he called to say I was on my way?"

"No one call. There be no phone."

"Then how…how do you know my name?"

"I know many things."

Tea sloshed from the glass. More rattled than he wanted to admit, Ben dried the spill with his fingers and wiped his hand down his pant leg. Spooky. Down-right spooky. Sylvester, curled beside him, switched his tail and stared at him with green eyes the size of emeralds. *The witch and her cat.* That's it. He'd had enough. He stood to go.

"The jaguar and the girl be one-in-the-same."

Ben sank back into the chair.

Chapter 9

Long eyelashes closed over dark eyes. Tibatha passed her hands over the cards in front of her and mumbled something Ben couldn't understand. Eyes opened, and she lit the white candle sitting beside her. The soothing scent of vanilla circled the room.

"White be for purity and protection, plus it smell good. I invite all angels and my peoples long past to come and help tell meaning of the cards."

The tarot deck was dog-eared and the pictures faded. She touched each card with the same care as a mother comforting a crying baby. Every nerve in Ben's body hummed. Fine hairs on the back of his arm stood straight up. Ears buzzed. Light-headed, he took a gulp of air. Tibatha placed a small stone in his hand. Brown with golden swirls.

"You feel the energy coming. Hold the Tiger-eye. The dizziness will pass."

Ben opened his mouth to speak. Her hand shot before him and she placed a ringed finger gently to his lips.

"Wait. Not all be here."

Sylvester's gaze traveled the kitchen. Up the walls. Down the walls. Around the cupboards. In the corners. Every so often he'd utter a hoarse meow. Amused, Ben followed his movements. A few moments passed before the orange tomcat blinked and lowered his head.

She chuckled. "They all here now. Cousin Tullie never on time. She late to own funeral, too."

In spite of himself, Ben laughed.

"The cards be old friends. They tell everything. They not judge. You ask all questions. None be foolish. Everything important. Understand?"

Ben nodded.

Tibatha flashed a smile that could melt lead. "Cousin Tullie say, it ok to breathe."

Heat crawled up the back of his neck. Unaware he'd been holding his breath, he let it out in one deep sigh.

Her playful mood sobered. She threw the first card.

The High Priestess.

A second card followed.

The Moon.

An all-knowing smile crossed her lips, and she leaned back against the padded cushion in her chair.

"It is as I suspect. The girl you seek be a daughter of the Howling Moon."

Confused, Ben waited for more. No words came.

"I don't understand," he said. "Thought I'd heard of every kind of moon there is. Full. Half. Crescent. Blue. Never a howling moon."

"No one can predict a Howling Moon," she answered.

"Go on," Ben prompted.

Tibatha's words came slow in a sing-song melody. Mesmerized by the smooth rhythm, Ben's breath again stuttered.

"A Howling Moon happen when the four elements—earth, air, fire, and water—the spirit of the sun, moon, the stars, all Gods and Goddesses join together as one and walk the earth in human man form.

On that night the moon shine deep purple and red, like a big ripe juicy plum ready to be picked from the midnight sky before it split apart. A moon so beautiful, it capture the soul and bubble the blood. A moon so powerful, one must surrender to its call to run and dance in its magic or lose the mind."

He didn't know what to think. What to say. Never heard of such a thing. The fan droned on and the faint sound of soft music came from a radio in the other room. He caught the grassy scent of sage. The fortune teller waited. For what? He didn't know. Maybe for him.

"Why? Why do they become human?"

She nodded, satisfied. Guess he'd asked the right question.

"To join with a mortal woman."

Not the answer he expected.

"Why?"

"To conceive a daughter."

Again, nothing like he'd imagined.

"Always a girl? Never a son?"

"Always a daughter of the Howling Moon."

He was tired of playing twenty questions. "Tell me all of it."

"Tullie say the same thing."

He was beginning to like the invisible cousin.

"Is always a girl child. Woman's heart be govern by compassion, love. Man's heart is too often ruled by hate, by violence." Her dark eyes gleamed at him. "You know of what I speak."

Yeah, he knew all too well.

"A daughter of the Howling Moon be conceived for a need, a purpose. She half spirit, half-mortal so she able to walk between dimensions. Most time she born with the gift of second Sight."

"So, the missing girl isn't Wayne's daughter at all but of this Howling Moon? Where does the jaguar fit in?"

"The black panther be her symbol. Her totem. The jaguar means reclaiming of one's true power and be linked to the feminine energy of the moon. This animal have great *mojo*…magic, much inner knowing, much power. If threatened—if in mortal danger—she summon the essence of the jungle cat deep inside her and transform into jaguar herself."

Lord Almighty. In all of his thirty-six years, he'd heard some far-fetched stories but nothing like this, yet he couldn't deny Wayne had been ripped to shreds by something. Still, to believe in a shape-shifting girl with the power of the universe at her beck and call was asking more of him than he could give. The heat from Tibatha's gaze made him sweat. Unable to match her stare, he racked his brain for something to say.

"You said the child of the Howling Moon was born for a reason. A need. So, what's this girl's purpose?"

Leaning forward, Tibatha threw the third card.

Justice.

She gazed up at him under heavy lashes. "To right a wrong."

"What kind of wrong?"

She flipped over a fourth card.

The Devil.

Ben's blood chilled. He had no idea why.

Tibatha's creamy face twisted into a frown, and she pitched another card.

The Tower.

One eyebrow cocked.

Not sure of what was going on, Ben tapped the two cards with his finger. "I don't like the looks of these. Judging from your puckered brow, neither do you. Tell me what they mean."

She answered by pulling yet three more cards from the deck. All *Pages*. Sylvester's throat hummed with a low growl. Ben reached over and gave the cat's head a reassuring pat. "Well?"

Her hand reached for the deck. Ben's temper snapped.

"Enough! No more cards. I've sat here and listened to your mumbo-jumbo for the last half-hour. You gotta know how hard it is for me to believe. I only came here as a favor to the Sheriff. For some reason he holds you and your beliefs in high regard which is mighty peculiar as he doesn't strike me as the supernatural type." His tone softened but held its bite. "I mean no disrespect, but it's all too strange."

Tibatha's voice was neither harsh nor angry. More like a mother's, soothing a child in need of a nap. "And so. The true Benjamin Sol finally appears. The no-nonsense, straight-to-the-point, jaded Benjamin Sol who be conflicted between good and evil. Him stomach burn and sting from the acid of doubt and guilt. I care not what you don't believe. What more important be what you do." She placed a dark hand on his chest and pressed. "So I wonder, Benjamin Sol. What secrets be in thine heart?"

She didn't wait for an answer.

"Sheriff Buford be good man with an open mind. He not understand all, but he willing to consider things that be beyond normal. The strange, as you say. I ask you. What be the difference between a Mexican jaguar in the swamps of Louisiana and a burning bush not consumed in the Hebrew mountain? Just because is strange, do not mean it not real."

Stunned, Ben couldn't think of one thing to say. There was more to this mysterious woman than met the eye. Majestic *and* intelligent. He felt a sheepish grin tug at the corner of his mouth.

"You sound like Mom."

He could tell by the gleam in her eye that this didn't surprise her. Tibatha scooted her chair back and returned to the ice box. She carried the pitcher to the table. The simple beauty of charcoal dark hands against the royal blue glass didn't go unnoticed to him as she refilled the jelly jar. A slight pat on his shoulder eased the frustration ready to burst from his chest.

"Cousin Tullie say, your mama have great love for you. And the other. Even though she was not her own."

A small sigh. "Danielle—Danni, was her stepdaughter. My stepsister."

"They both at peace now and ask, when will you be?"

Ben shrugged and scratched Sylvester's ears. Damned if he liked where the conversation was headed. Tibatha was fixing to rip open old wounds that time had scared over. "This isn't about me." His voice carried more acid than he intended. "What did those cards mean?"

It was her turn to sigh. "A great wickedness come to claim the children."

Alarmed, Ben shot up and paced the room. "What kind of wickedness?"

"I know not. But it be from one who claim to be what they not."

"Jedidiah Wayne."

"You quick to say this name. Why be that?"

Ben shook his head. "I don't know. I said it before I thought."

"The Knowing work that way."

"So do coincidences."

"There be no such things."

Surprised that he was more amused at her retort than annoyed, he paced over to the window and touched the crystal hanging there. Blue, green, and red sparkles danced in the sunlight. Truth was this smooth-talking fortune teller was growing on him. He liked her confidence and calm manner even though he'd bet, just like the gators that hid beneath the serene surface of the water, if riled, she'd snap you in half. He turned back to face her, his hands gripped the lip of the chipped porcelain sink behind him.

"Let me get all this straight. This daughter of the Howling Moon was born to protect the children. To stop wickedness. Let me ask *you,* Lady Tibatha, even if I buy this fantastic story, how is a sixteen-year-old girl going to that?"

"Great power will come at The Shimmering."

Lord Almighty. More hoodoo-voodoo talk. He sighed heavy, pulled out a chair, and settled his long frame onto it. What the hell? He'd already spent an hour here what was one more? Besides, it was too hot to run around in the swamps. Better to go in the cool of the morning. He took a sip of tea and glanced at Tibatha through the plain glass.

"Ok. I'll bite. What the hell is The Shimmering?"

Chapter 10

Tibatha's deep laugh surprised him.

"Tullie say, to explain The Shimmering to this pretty mon this sexy mon, be like wringing blood from a turnip. Not possible."

Ben's laugh wasn't so merry. "Humor me."

Ebony eyes speared him to the chair. Sweat popped on his forehead, crawled down his neck and made his armpits itch. She continued to study him like he was a bug trapped under glass. Well, he'd played poker with the best of them. If she thought he'd be the first to blink, she had another think coming. Ice-blue locked with glazed onyx. Her eyebrow arched. Oh hell. Who was he fooling? She knew damned well it took every ounce of his being not to look away.

The room darkened. The sun must've ducked behind the clouds. For some reason, he shivered. Tibatha pressed her dark chocolate hands together in front of her lips, and Ben braced himself for some sort of pagan prayer or chanting. Instead, she gazed deep into his eyes and spoke slow and direct.

"The Shimmering most magical. Most reverent. Most mysterious." Her fingers laced together and she chose her words with care. "It be an anointing. An awakening. A recalling of the omniscience each of us by birth possesses but have forgotten—an absolute knowing rather than mere believing that all things be possible.

"The girl have no knowledge of her destiny. But the night fast approaches when all will change. For reasons she not know, she be pulled to cast the sacred circle, stand in its center, and bring down the moon deep into her soul."

Her hands flew apart and her eyes glowed with excitement. "It be like she swallow the silver orb whole and its radiant power and glory shimmer around and from her much like heat waves rising from hot pavement."

Caught by her passion and force, Ben's heart raced. Lord Almighty. He wanted to believe. Truly he did. Sweat trickled from his brow and he reached to wipe it away. His fingers brushed against the star pinned on his chest, and he froze.

The star—his badge— was a constant reminder of the vow he'd sworn over Danni's lifeless body. A promise for redemption. For justice. Was it coincidence that he and the girl were after the same thing? To right a wrong? Protect the innocent? Was it mere chance that brought him to this backwoods hick town, or fate? Shit. What was he thinking? There was no such thing as fate. All this hocus-pocus talk had him rattled. His head throbbed.

He reached in this pocket for the yellow tin of Anacin. Popped three headache pills in his mouth. Tibatha watched every move but sat in silence. The tarot deck rested in front of him. On a whim, he flipped over the top card.

The Knight of Swords.

He studied the picture of the young man dressed in armor aside a white horse, sword drawn, bravely charging head first into unknown danger and smiled. "I like this one."

"And well you should," Tibatha whispered. "For it be you."

She leaned back and clicked her tongue against pearl-white teeth. "You will search the wilds but not find the girl unless she deem it so, however, you will feel her essence always surround you. She be in every blade of grass. Every drop of rain. Every tree. Every leaf. For the wilds of nature be her home. Her sanctuary. Her church. But there be one thing you must always remember."

"What's that?"

"She human. She not immortal. At times, she fragile as thin crystal glass. During these times, she most vulnerable. And it is at these moments evil will strike. She will need a protector—a knight—to ground her, to save her.

"Me?" Ben laughed.

Tibatha's easy going manner dissolved and her voice roared. "Do not make fun of things you know nothing about. This I say true. One day she will need a champion, and she will call to you."

Lightning fast, Tibatha's hand shot across the table and grabbed his wrist in a vice-tight grip. She threw words hard as rocks.

"And when that day come, Benjamin Sol, you *will* believe."

Time stretched a country mile between them. The urge to tell her how wrong she was, itched something fierce, but he dare not scratch.

She broke the hold, rose from the chair, and stomped into the other room. Probably reached her limit with his cynicism and sarcasm and was unlocking the door getting ready to throw him out. Her low humming and the opening of a drawer told him different. She returned and handed him a small red-colored bag.

He turned it over in his hand. "What's this?"

"In Voudoun religion it called a *gris-gris* bag. Wear around neck, next to skin. It will protect you."

Ben stood and patted his holster. "No offense, but I got all the protection I need right here."

Her haunting laugh unnerved him. Uneasy, he shifted from one foot to the other.

"It not to protect you from the things you can see and shoot, but from the things you cannot."

She took his hand in hers and led him to the door. "Sol mean the sun. The light. Go. Find the girl. Do not doubt what I say." She twirled him around to face her.

"The light must destroy the dark."

Chapter 11

I woke with a pounding in my head. Feeling like thousands of tiny frosted spider feet were crawling up the side of my face, pain spread from my jawbone to below my eye. If I dared remove my hand pressed against my tingling cheek, my face would break and slide right off. My lip, swolled up bigger than a horny toad, oozed blood. There was only one other time Jedidiah had backhanded me so hard, the same cold day when I'd cut through Granny LeBeaux's yard on my way home from school.

When my stiff fingers couldn't handle the cold no more, I dropped my arithmetic book. The book and my red Big Chief tablet slid downhill and landed smack-dab in the middle of the ice that covered the stock pond. I held my breath and listened to the thin ice crack and pop. Ever so slow, the splintered ice inched and split until the pond looked like one of those fancy lace tablecloths the church women put out for the Easter and Christmas dinners. Scared if I stepped out, the ice would break into thousands of pieces and I'd slip and freeze under the water, I refused to place one toe on that slippery surface. Jedidiah overheard me asking Mama for a nickel for another tablet. Hollarin' at the top of his lungs, quoting scripture from the book of John about how wastefulness was a sin, he hit me so hard upside the head, my teeth rattled and my right ear buzzed for a week.

At least this time I could hear, but every muscle screamed as I climbed down Grandpa Cypress. Stiff, sore, and clumsy as a box turtle on its back, I tripped over the carpet bag lying at his feet. I gawked at the satchel. Where had it come from? Didn't remember grabbing it. But then again, some details of what had happened before I woke up on Grandpa's thick arm were a might fuzzy. Still clutching my cheek, I picked up the bag and staggered further into the wild. My throat burned with a powerful thirst. Good thing I knew where to find fresh water.

If you didn't know where the spring was, you'd never find it. I stumbled across it by accident the summer before when I'd followed a trail of paw prints into the brush. I figured I'd see a sleek, yellow cougar or a tufted-eared bobcat at the end of the path. Instead, right in the middle of the Louisiana swamp, I found the Garden of Eden.

Always shaded under a roof of cypress and magnolia branches, the rocked pool gave drink and comfort to everything that crawled, walked, slithered, or flew in the swamp. Flowers the color of the rainbow, green, lush bushes and ferns of every size and shape surrounded and stood guard over the unlikely oasis.

No matter how hot, muggy and sultry the air, coolness surrounded the pool. Next to Grandpa Cypress, the spring was my favorite place to run to when the day burned with fever and soured my mood. I could smell its rain-fresh scent seconds before I flopped on my belly and gulped down buckets of its sweetness. The girl under the mirrored surface scared the dickens out of me.

The bruised and battered image under the water couldn't be me. Hair so matted and full of twigs and leaves, rats would've refused to nest in it, swirled tangled around a black and blue stained face. Crusted blood clung to chin and lips. Still leery of the reflection, I touched my cheek. The watery likeness winced. Dried blood under chipped, broken fingernails made me gasp. That's when everything that happened the night before reared back and kicked me full in the gut knocking the wind plumb out of me. I crumbled to the ground and curled into a ball. Pictures flashed in my mind.

Mama's body. Jedidiah's bleeding face. A mighty jungle cat.

Something about that wild panther gnawed at me. I knew about every kind of animal there was. That cat was a jaguar and a long way from home. A cougar or bobcat in my bedroom, while strange, could still be explained but a jaguar? What was she doing in this neck of the woods? And why did I feel kinship to her?

Sometimes in school, Miss Hanagan gave what she called pop quizzes. I hated them something fierce. The shock of an unstudied test froze my brain. The correct answers would tease and dance just out of reach of my mind. I could almost touch the right reply before it would skitter away and vanish. The jaguar was like a pop test. Deep down, I knew why it was important, but for now the reason dangled just out of reach.

Swamp sounds of frogs croaking, birds squawking, and bugs buzzing surrounded me.

I laid beside the still waters swaddled in their comfort. Maybe if I didn't think about the jaguar, his meaning would come to me. I tucked the cat's face in a corner and turned my thinking to how good the cool, damp moss felt on my bruised cheek. Of how green and sweet the flowers and honeysuckle smelled. A whoosh of wings came up beside me and an egret landed within arm's reach. Still as a corpse, I held my breath and wondered at the grace and beauty of the gray bird. Just as easy as it had landed, the big bird lifted right off into flight as if God had plucked him up with an invisible hand. I sighed and shut my eyes. That's when the answer hit me.

The panther was me.

Chapter 12

My laugh sounded too loud underneath the lush canopy of branches and leaves. Folks couldn't change into animals. Again I gawked at blood-stained hands. Remembrance of warm flesh ripped from bone throbbed under broken fingernails. The rusty iron smell of fresh blood filled my nose. Wind in my face. Moist earth beneath my feet. Low growls in my throat.

Heart pounding, I jolted upright. A knowing deep down stirred and spread from head to toe. I wasn't thinkin' crazy. It was truth. I'd run through the dark with the heart and soul of the jungle cat.

And I owned the night.

Feelin' all mixed up inside, I sat so long without moving, my bones fused into one hard ache. Questions filled my head. How did I turn into a wild cat? Could I do it again? What other kinds of animals could I be? What about birds? Could I fly? Why did this happen? What was the reason? *What* was I?

Too many questions with no answers.

My belly growled. I pulled the carpet bag to me and rummaged inside. Candles, matches, a small quilt, clothes, Grandma's brush and comb, a heart locket, and a tin of crackers.

Bless you, Mama.

Mama.

The gold necklace caught the sun's rays and glowed

warm in my hand. Burning tears made me blink. Weren't never gonna see Mama ever again. Grief, big as a giant's fist, grabbed a hold of my heart and squeezed the last drop of air from my lungs.

What was I going to do? I had no place to run. Wouldn't in a hundred years go back home. Couldn't go to town. Jedidiah have folks keepin an eye out for me. Sarah Rose be hundreds of miles away. Aunt Hester ever see me again, she'd throttle me for sure and dance a jig on my grave.

Salty crackers, that just moments before were welcomed like manna from heaven, turned to a gummy ball in my mouth. Night was fixing to claim the swamp. I was alone with no shelter, and while I loved the wetlands it didn't mean I loved everything that crawled or slithered here. Worry pecked at me. Fear gnawed at my gut.

To chase the heebie-jeebies away, I plunged my head under the cool water and let icy fingers crawl up my neck and over my ears. Gulping for air, I straightened and washed the blood from my face. The cold spring water numbed the throbbing in my cheek. Cross-legged, I sat beside the pool, pulled fingers through tangled locks and willed myself to be still.

Don't think. Stare only at the glassy smoothness of the water until the swamp closes in tight and the light of day dims and blurs into lazy haze.

"You are never alone."

The voice, while lyrical and easy on the ear, crackled like a dry leather wallet being opened for the first time in a long time. A small woman with gray hair falling to the waist stood before me and smiled a toothless grin.

"I know you," I whispered. "You're Granny LeBeaux."

A witchy cackle sparked a glow into mischievous eyes. "And I have always known you, little Bethany Ann."

A shiver pushed the secret of that cold winter's day at the pond out of shadow into light. Something had happened that day that I'd never told anyone, not even Sarah Rose.

Jedidiah had forced me to go back for the book. Said he flat didn't care if I froze to death getting' it. Be one less mouth to feed. Mama begged him not to send me into the cold. She grabbed his arm to stop him from popping me another good one. He flung her to the floor like a ragdoll and shoved me out the door. I ran hard so's not to hear Mama's cries when she took the beating that belonged to me. Hate scratched and rolled around in my belly like a bag full of scrawny cats.

I'd kill him. Someday, I'd kill him.

By the time I got to the pond, ice-cold fear had turned to boiling anger. I could've melted every square inch of ice with one look, but I didn't have to. There on the frosted bank, wrapped in wax paper, was my Big Chief tablet and math book. Dry as bone. How? Who?

It all made sense now, and I smiled at the feisty little woman before me. "It was you, wasn't it? "That winter day? You saved my book and tablet. Why?"

"*Loa* say I must help the daughter of the Howling Moon."

"*Loa*?"

"In Voodoo, *Loa* is God."

"So I was right. You are a Voodoo priestess."

A tilt of her head one way. "Perhaps, yes." A tip of

her head the other way. "Perhaps, no." An impish grin. "But I have no shrunken heads today."

Never would've guessed Granny LeBeaux could be so playful. Shoot, me and Sarah Rose reckoned she'd be meaner than snake spit. That she stabbed voodoo dolls with long, sharp needles or whipped up spells in a cast-iron cauldron to hex folks. But she was really nice. I felt downright ashamed about thinkin' bad of her and ducked my head. Maybe I should tell her how sorry I was, but when I glanced up, the sound of merry chuckles was all that was left of her.

I ran after her airy figure that bobbed and weaved through the brush.

"*Loa* be everywhere. In the trees. In stone. Air. Water. Wind. Calm your fear and listen to what she speak. All questions come clear when the time is right."

"That's the second time you said that. What do you mean? What's fixin' to happen?"

"The Shimmering."

"What's that?"

"It's when you reclaim the power that is rightfully yours."

"What power?"

She didn't answer. Instead, she turned and faded into the wild. Her carefree elfish laughter trailed a few steps behind. "At the full moon, all will be revealed. Follow the path. *Loa* will provide."

Mist cleared and brightness surrounded me. I sat back at the pool. Hadn't moved an inch.

There wasn't one trace of Granny LeBeaux anywhere. No broken twigs. No footprints. Nothing betrayed her appearance. But that didn't surprise me none.

Granny LeBeaux had been dead for years.

Chapter 13

The vision left me light-headed. Never felt that way before. And the image was different than all the others I'd had too. More powerful. More real. What was Granny talking about? The Shimmering? What power was coming? Reckon it had something to do with being the daughter of the Howling Moon but for the life of me, I had no idea what. And now weren't the time to study on it anyway. Granny LeBeaux's message had been clear. *Follow the path.*

I gathered my things, but faltered when I stood up. Which way? A jolt of panic made me swallow hard. Eyes closed tight, I took a deep breath and settled into myself. Eyes opened and feet walked like they had a mind of their own. Deeper into the woods.

Deeper.

Deeper.

The bleached wood of the hut stuck out like a sore thumb in the middle of the green wildness. Not truly believing what I saw, I walked on tiptoes to the front of the shack, climbed up the steps, and peeked inside. Being so quiet was downright stupid. It was plain to see no one lived in the place. The screen door moaned when I stepped inside. Only two rooms. Dirt, dust, cobwebs everywhere. I glanced up. No daylight leaked through the roof and there were screens on the windows and a strong front door. Small but safe.

A rocking chair sat in the corner of the biggest room, a wood stove and table in the tiny kitchen. Not knowing what could be curled up inside the oven, I flung open the door and jumped back. A nest of leaves and twigs had once been home to some kind of critter but was empty now. Miracles of miracles, a full coal-oil lamp sat on one of the window sills and canned goods lined the shelf.

I blew dust off a can of the peaches and rummaged through the single cabinet. Praise be. A knife, fork, and can opener. Taking the food to the front porch, I sat on the steps and wolfed down the fruit. The peaches tasted sweeter than any cherry licorice whip ever bought in Baker's Emporium. Mind full of the jagged edge, I carefully tipped the can to my mouth and guzzled the sugary juice.

Sitting so deep in the belly of the swamp, night fell quicker and darker. I lit one of Mama's candles and returned to the porch steps. The candlelight twinkled like a fairy's eye through the black. Night sounds of the wetlands wrapped round me, cricket chirps, frog grunts, ever now and again the eerie hoots of an owl. A half-eyed moon played tag with the tree tops and bobbed through the branches. Granny LeBeaux's words came back to me. "*Loa* be everywhere. Listen to what she speak." What was the Voodoo God telling me?

"Home," the soft breeze answered.

Bone tired, I padded the rocking chair with Mama's quilt and curled into it like a kitten. Tomorrow, I'd clean the place best I could. Maybe find a way to haul water from the spring back here. Nobody, not even Sarah Rose, would believe these last couple of days. Had a hard time coming to terms with it myself. And if what Granny LeBeaux had said about The Shimmering,was true, whatever that be, more was fixing to happen. Eyes heavy, I fell into deep sleep.

"Bethany Ann…Bethany Ann…We're under here…Can you hear our cries?"

A young girl's voice, tiny and full of tears moaned long and slow. A dead fishy odor soaked the air. Slimly pond reeds wove through flaxen hair that floated around a bloated face, pasty white with empty, dark eyes. A second body, puffy, bulging, naked drifted with the current. Tender young flesh, bloody and raw, food for fish and crab.

"Bethany Ann…Bethany Annnnn…Save us."

Purplish-blue hands, swollen bare feet, large eyes void of all life, filled only with eternal fear. Lips blown up big as circus balloons, cried out over and over sounding like haints wailing into the wind through the blackness of still night.

"Bethany Ann…hear our cries. In the dim light of early dawn he held us, not wrapped in loving arms but under the water instead."

A small bony hand grabbed and tore at the pond scum weeds, desperate to touch something, anything alive. "We are trapped, doomed for eternity in our watery graves. Free us."

Faces, hair, black eyes, fear, death, forever circling. Forever reaching and not finding. Voices, pleading, begging, "Bethany Ann…find Benjamin. Set us free."

I woke from the dream wringing wet. A small breeze floated past the front door and I stumbled into its coolness, retching with each step. Couldn't shake the feel of clammy, squishy hands on my body. The moldy, wet burlap smell of rotting flesh from my nose. The sight of water snakes gilding through empty eye sockets from my mind. A shiver raced up my spine. A squirming in my gut made me clutch my belly and lean against the dewy wetness of the cabin's wall. Breath came short and choppy.

What was happening to me? My visions never made me sick before.

Dawn spread through the wilds smooth as butter on warm toast. Loud-mouthed crows hollered at the daylight with loud caws, and blue jays yelled thief right back at them. Most nightmares shun the light, but this one held tight. Then again, this was no mere dream, but rather a forewarning of things to come.

Didn't have the slightest notion who Benjamin was. But I knew the girls. Recognized their ghostly-white faces. Remembered their names.

And Jedidiah Wayne had killed them all.

Chapter 14

A week passed. The bloated faces that had haunted and woeful cries that had chilled faded into nothingness as well, but the spooky feeling of the night terror lingered. Never before afraid to shut my eyes and wait for dreams to slip in and out of shadows, I fought to stay awake, working until bone weary.

I found an old bucket out back of the cabin and hauled water two, maybe three times a day from the spring. On hands and knees, I scrubbed and rubbed till the little place shined up like a new penny. Keeping one eye peeled for gators, I managed to hook a few perch and catfish with a cane pole, a shoestring from my boot, and a safety pin.

All-in-all, things weren't bad during the day. But after the sun went down, loneliness threw a heavy coat over my shoulders. With only the dim glow of the lantern's flame for company and the voices of crickets and frogs to listen to, my thoughts often turned to Mama. Missed her something fierce. Sometimes when the aching got so bad, I'd lean into the cabin wall, and pretend I snuggled next to her warmth. If I squeezed my teary eyes shut real hard, I could hear her soft whisper in my ear.

"Hush, child. Mama's here."

I loved those moments.

Too often, however, thoughts of Mama caused

Jedidiah's wicked face to jump before me. The memory of his pawing hands and skunk breath overpowered the clean scent of magnolia and honeysuckle. Caused my heart to bang against my chest and hate to sear my belly. Those times, sleep never came.

Those times, I slammed the cabin door shut, jammed the rocker under the knob, and sat huddled in the corner until dawn. Those times I weren't alone. Fear sat beside me. If Jedidiah ever catch me, he'd skin me alive, torture me, like a cat torments a mouse before ripping its little heart out. I'd escaped once, but would I be so lucky the next time? Could I summon the jungle cat curled at the bottom of my spine to rise up and strike again?

Those moments, I hated.

But for the most part, I liked my tiny haven nestled in the deep wild. I took each day as it came and tried not to fret on things that may never come to pass. Even so, an uneasy feeling began to build in the pit of my stomach. A restlessness I couldn't explain, nagged me, made sleep dang near impossible.

Something big was fixing to happen.

Dawn birthed a day steamy as a pot of boiling crawdads. Everything stank like a drawer full of dirty, sweaty socks. Tired, out-of-sorts, and sweating bullets, I did nothing all day. Didn't fetch water, gather berries, fish, nothing but sit and stew in my own juice. I shucked off my overalls and walked around, wearing only a shirt with sleeves rolled up to my armpits and underwear. Mama probably be rolling in her grave, but it weren't like anybody was gonna see me.

Long after supper time when twilight sneaks in and steals the day, everything changed.

Right off I noticed the smell. Air, ripe with the

promise of rain, dissolved the putrid, stagnant stink into baby-fresh sweetness. The second thing that caught my attention was the sky.

I ain't never seen the ocean. Chances were good that I never would. But I think the way the sky looks when a storm is brewing would be a kissing cousin to the churning salty water. Clouds, some pearly white, others faded gray, rolled and tumbled much like I supposed waves beating against the shore would.

Completely at the mercy of the wind, clouds took on a life of their own, and changed into overgrown shapes and sizes. A big fluffy pillow here. A giant angel wing there. My favorites were the ones that looked like huge dog tongues just waiting to lap up the rain when it fell.

The closer the storm moved in, the more the clouds and sky resembled my idea of the ocean. No longer soft and fluffy, but fierce and dark, clouds raced across the sky like roaring water. Billowy feather pillows curled into mighty fists of God that shook their power at the earth. Wind turned stronger.

Cool air breathed life back into the bayou—and me.

My insides crackled and popped with reined-in excitement. Reminded me of Uncle Ezekiel's coon dogs right before a hunt. Them hounds would work themselves into a madness howling, baying and struggling against ropes that held tight, just itching to catch the scent and run. At that moment, I understood. Felt like a teakettle ready to blow. I bolted from the porch and ran crazy wild.

Blood raced like liquid fire through my veins. Eyes, sharp as tacks, pierced the dark. Jumped over a log like a deer. Trees whizzed past. Lightning tore up the sky behind me.

Faster.

Faster.

The more I ran, the more I craved the wind in my hair and the sound of blood throbbing in my ears. Unexplained joy bubbled up from deep inside me, and I laughed like a loon into the dark. I burst into a clearing and stopped dead in my tracks. Heart pounding, I sucked in air.

A yearning—no, it were more than that—a calling forced me to draw a circle in the dirt and stand firm in its center. Cool then warm wind bent trees to the ground and snapped them back into place but rooted in that circle, the breeze calmed and caressed my face gentle as a mother's touch.

Eyes shut, head back, arms straight out from my sides, I twirled. Around and around. Twirled like a little girl in the mist and wind until deep in my bones I knew with one leap I could fly. Rain beat the earth in sheets. Yet, I stood strong in its fury, dry as bone. Streaks of yellow lightning ripped the sky apart at the seams. Unafraid, I dared it closer. Jesus, God. The whole bayou had exploded into a wild, foaming-at-the-mouth frenzy.

Then, everything stopped.

Eyes wide, I gawked at the sky.

God Almighty. Thunder had done knocked the moon from heaven, and it had landed right in front of me.

Maybe poets or really good writers could think up words that could describe the splendor of this moon, but I didn't know a single one. Beautiful? Not pretty enough. Huge? Not big enough. So close, yet so far away, I ached to reach out and touch its glow.

The more I stared, the closer the silver orb came.

Closer.

My heart damn near stopped.
Closer.
My breath did .
Closer.
I fell to my knees

Surrounded in silver radiance, I raised my arms in reverence to the strength and majesty that throbbed like a heartbeat deep within the shining globe. A sharp, pining howl rang through the crystal clear night. Took a moment to realize the sound came from me.

Once, just for fun, Sarah Rose cracked a hen's egg on the top of my head. Slimy, gooey yolk crawled ever-so-slow down my face and neck and soaked into my skin. Just like that egg, the moon burst open and anointed me with its life…its power…its glory. I gulped down its essence.

Every inch of my being hummed like I swallowed a hornet's nest. A dazzling glow turned dark skin into brilliance. All around me a shimmering light danced like hundreds of silver ribbons in the midnight sky.

Doubts and guessing stopped. Knowing began.

In the natural beauty of raw wildness, encircled by God's light and supremacy, I stood reborn. Baptized by the pureness of rain and earth, wind and fire into the Church of the Howling Moon.

Chapter 15

Crisp leaves crunched beneath heavy combat boots. Trees, naked and foreboding, reached out with pencil-thin fingers, grabbed at the uniform jacket, tried to hold him back. Deep in his gut panic swirled, rose up to choke, to smother him. He fought the urge to bolt reckless and headstrong away from the woods. Willed himself to walk steady. Focus his mind. Quit thinking.

But he knew.

He knew before the damp fall air carried the scent of decay. Before the shadows of black-winged scavengers circling above drew him from the beaten path into the wooded thickness.

He knew.

"Danni?"

Footsteps turned to lead. What was wrong? His feet didn't work. Empty inside, he sank to his knees.

Oh, God. No.

All he could do was stare. Gawk at white limp arms and the dark maroon slash marks that defiled her tiny wrists. The blood that stained the leaves and grass a rusty red. At hollow green eyes, glazed smooth as marbles. At the razor blade.

Benjamin woke from tortured sleep and struggled from the tangle of sheets wrapped round long legs. The single flat pillow sailed across the room. Retching, cursing, he staggered to the bathroom, barely making it in time before he threw up everything but his toenails.

Sweat-soaked, hands trembling, he fumbled with the faucets and stood under the shower head until cold water washed the dark memory of that awful day down the drain.

Damn nightmare was always the same. The outcome, always the same. Even after weeks of therapy with the base shrink, even after fighting a world war, those vacant green eyes never yielded. Never stopped haunting him.

If eyes were the windows to the soul, then Danni's spirit was hollow, black as sin. Why? If the Church was to be believed, it was the price to pay for suicide. But he didn't believe in Church doctrines or even God for that matter, so after all these years the answer to the question still eluded him. Still tormented him.

He dried off, tied the rough towel around his waist, and shuffled into the tiny kitchen. Soon the fresh aroma and the gurgling of percolated coffee flooded the room. He grabbed the box of Sugar Frosted Flakes from the counter and glared at Tony the Tiger's beaming orange-and-white face.

"What are you grinning at?"

Tony didn't answer, just continued to mock him with his broad cardboard smile.

"Yeah, well, can't blame you. Guess life on a cereal box *is* pretty happy compared to life in the real world. After all, people don't kill themselves in the Land of Cornflakes."

God, he was pissy this morning. Arguing with a cereal box? Could he get any more surly?

He tore open the box lid and fought with the wax paper inside. Tough as nails, the pressed seal refused to split apart.

"Son-of-a-bitch!"

He threw the box of frosted flakes across the room. Tony the Tiger hit the refrigerator with a dull thud and slumped to the floor.

"Not feeling so grrrrrreat now, are ya?"

Oh yeah, he could get a lot more cynical.

Outside the first streaks of light painted the eastern sky a brilliant orange and yellow. Good day as any to go the swamp. Hell, he'd just thrown a tiger across the room, facing a jaguar would be a piece of cake. Plus the way his day had gone so far, he was in a perfect mood to shoot something.

He pulled on his uniform and buckled the .357 around his waist. The red *gris-gris* bag fell from his pocket. The urge to throw the good luck charm in the trash tempted him. He kicked it under the bed and stomped out the door.

The untamed beauty of the swamp surprised him. The greenness. The vivid colors. Tall skinny trees draped in bolts of Spanish moss flared out into skirts of hollow wood. Waterways ranging from deep blue to mossy green wove through and around cypress trees bent and twisted like pretzels in a jar.

But he was no fool. Danger lurked around every corner. Alligators. Snakes. Mosquitos big enough to throw a saddle on and ride. Ugly, evil looking swamp rats bigger than a dog with razor sharp teeth that could tear flesh from bone in minutes. If a jaguar had the guts to hang out here, more power to him.

The hair on the back of his neck pricked. Four years of combat kicked in. His hand tightened around the .357's butt. Someone was following him. He whirled.

Nothing.

Spooky damn swamp gave him the willies. He should go back. There wasn't any jungle cat here.

Guilt nagged him. What about Wayne's missing daughter? All that crap Lady Tibatha told him about the girl being a daughter of the Howling Moon was just that…crap. What if the girl was out here, alone and hurt? He'd turned his back on Danni when she needed help and it cost her life. Damned if he'd have another set of innocent eyes plaguing his sleep. He trudged deeper into the bayou.

Throat felt like he'd swallowed a bale of cotton.

Stupid not to bring a canteen.

His belly growled.

Should've eaten those flakes instead of throwing them across the kitchen.

Dammit! Every tree and path looked the same.

All confused. Which way to go?

What was wrong with him, making such rookie mistakes? He knew better.

Lightheaded. Befuddled. Dehydrated. Where in this bitter sweet wetland maze of great beauty and creeping danger could he find fresh water? Thirsty, hungry, and fuzzy-minded, his head pounded. He couldn't think. And if that damn crow didn't shut up, he was going to put a bullet right between its beady eyes.

When the loud-mouthed bird sailed to the ground right in front of him, Benjamin froze in his tracks. Close enough to reach out and touch, the crow stood firm, cocked his head, and let out a screech that would wake the dead. Blue-black feathers gleamed in the sunlight and dark eyes studied him with both curiosity and great intensity. Amused, Benjamin could almost see the wheels turning in the bird's head. What was he thinking? Another ear-splitting squawk. Wonder where he got fresh water? As if on cue, the crow lifted off.

Benjamin kept his gaze trained on the bird and followed its flight. Deeper into the bayou, through the thick brush, around the bend, and there it was.

The spring.

Cold clear water soothed his raw throat. Every deep gulp pumped life back into tissue and muscles. He plunged his head under the surface and stayed there until his lungs screamed and he straightened. Smoothing back his hair, Benjamin let the water crawl down his neck and back.

Bone weary, he leaned back against a cypress and closed his eyes. Shadowed coolness wrapped round him. He'd rest for a while—just a short while, then hike back to the jeep. An obnoxious caw-caw sounded above him. He smiled.

"Thanks, buddy. I owe you one."

He fell into a deep sleep.

The sound of beating drums jolted him wide awake.

Chapter 16

Damn. How long had he been sleeping?

Humid and steamy, the marshland still baked from the sun's rays, but light had slipped into twilight sleep. No flashlight. No lantern. Hell, not even a damn match. *Got to get out of here.*

He couldn't move.

The ground vibrated from the beating sound, shook his spine, and hummed in his head. Lethargic, slow-minded, he wanted to resist the drum's hypnotic tug but had no will to fight.

Ever-so-slowly he rose and followed the thumping sound. Trancelike. Branches and moss tore at his legs. Mosquitoes buzzed his ears. Didn't matter. The pounding demanded obedience.

He walked deeper into falling night.

The scent of wood smoke reached his nose before the orange pinprick of light cut the dark. Spellbound, he leaned against the smooth red-brown bark of a five-story bald cypress and gawked.

Dark-skinned men and women paced around a huge black cauldron resting on the coals of a roaring fire. The squawks of terrified chickens ripped the night apart and the smell of burnt feathers hung thick in the damp air. During the war he'd seen worse carnage than a sacrificed rooster but for some reason his belly pitched and rolled at the thought and stink of a boiled-alive chicken.

The drumming quickened. So did his pulse.

Writhing and thrashing, dark bodies flailed to the madding beat. Sweat-drenched skin gleamed like burnt copper in the light of golden flames. Benjamin's heart matched the frenzied tempo, slamming against his chest, ready to burst. A river of sweat ran down his back. Dizzy, sick to his stomach, he struggled to draw a full breath in air heavy as guilt and still as death.

Thirty voices chanted as one, calling out a summons to the dark night.

Goose bumps popped on every bare inch of skin. He'd experienced blind, petrifying fear in battle but this feeling of dark spooky anticipation flooding his body was something quite different. In many ways more terrifying.

A woman dressed in a flowing white gown appeared out of the steamy mist and gyrated to the wild beat. Jerking. Convulsing. Pulled and twisted every which way like a witchy-haired marionette tied to an invisible string. Bending to the ground she grabbed a handful of dirt. Reverent. Solemn. She raised her cupped hands to the blue-black sky. A sudden wind stirred the leaden air, swept the offering from her grasp and scattered the dust to the four corners. North. South. East. West. Charcoal hair whipped around her face. Skin, wet and slick, glistened in the heat and flames. Lifting her arms to the diamond-pointed stars she clapped her hands three times and brought down the power of the gods.

Thunder boomed and echoed like cannon fire through the brush and trees.

Knocked to his knees, Ben ducked and covered his ears with trembling hands.

A bolt of lightning ripped the heavens in half and hit

the ground with light so bright his eyes burned and teared. The rotten-egg smell of sulfur wrinkled his nose. Claps of thunder cracked sharp as a bullwhip and lashed the ground.

From deep inside the white-hot flash a body took shape. An arm. A leg. Unfolding like a blow-up doll at a carnival, the figure straightened, drew a long ragged breath and stepped forth. Skin dark as glazed onyx. Coarse wiry hair like black barbed wire. Naked. Muscular. Undulating.

Mesmerized, Benjamin watched the figure join with the woman. Their dance was one of raw, untamed sexuality.

Heated.

Lovemaking without touching.

Sinful.

Beautiful.

They swayed together, created a spell of intoxicating energy that shot out and seized Benjamin's heart. He gasped for air.

Her flowing gown plastered to a slender, lithe body, the Voodoo Priestess broke the spell. Graceful. Giving the illusion of floating, she glided to the middle of the circle. Drums beat the air with fierce, violent fists. Dancers joined hands, leaned their soaking wet bodies into the circle then out. Chanting, singing, rocking back and forth.

The Priestess opened the lid on a long box.

He swallowed hard.

A coffin.

The snake she lifted out was way longer than he was tall and as big around as his thick leg.

Sensual. Seductive. She draped the python around

the entity's broad shoulders. Tongue flicking, broad head swaying, the reptile curled around a thick neck and gazed into eyes dark and empty as the grave. Without hesitation the being opened his mouth, uncurled a black tongue and licked the serpent's glossy skin like a lover's neck.

Every nerve in Ben's body hummed. All consciousness narrowed down to a single thought. He had to get closer. The fire. The sweat. The air thick with reckless abandon boiled his blood. An uncontrollable force yanked him from his knees.

He took a step.

The hand on his arm stopped him cold.

Afraid of what he would find, he turned and gazed up into eyes the color of indigo. The girl's voice cut through the numbing fog in his head.

"You do not belong here."

The grip on his hand, strong as iron, pulled him away from the drums. From the chanting. From the dance. Broke the hypnotic spell that like a drug stole away all thought, strength, and feeling.

Inky darkness surrounded the swamp. He couldn't see a thing. Completely at the mercy of this wisp of a girl, his hand sweated inside hers as he stumbled behind her. How strange. The dark didn't bother her. Sure-footed, confident, she wove through the maze of bushes, ferns, and trees without missing a step.

Must have eyes like a cat.

A beacon of yellow lantern flame shone through the clear night. Only when they'd climbed up the porch steps of the little shack did she let go of his hand. Exhausted, he leaned against the wooden rail.

"Drink."

He took the tin can from her hand and tilted it to dry

lips. She sat Indian-style across from him and waited. He wiped his mouth on the back of his hand and gazed at her face. Pretty eyes. Deep purple. Funny pupils. Shaped like a crescent moon.

"You're her, aren't you? Jedidiah Wayne's daughter?"

"I be no kin to Jedidiah Wayne."

Oh yeah, right. Daughter of the Howling Moon. How could he forget? He shook his head. Hell, after what he'd just seen, that notion didn't seem so farfetched anymore.

"I'm Bethany Ann."

He nodded. "My name's—"

"Benjamin."

He couldn't help the deep sigh. A few hours ago it would've rattled his cage good that she knew his name. But after a night of voodoo priestesses, monster snakes, and conjured spirits nothing could shock him anymore.

"Haints told me you'd come."

Oh hell. He was wrong.

Chapter 17

"You look a might peaked there, Benjamin."

She disappeared into the cabin and returned with an open can of peaches. "Don't look like much, but they'll hit the spot."

Half-hearted, he bit into a slice and felt the sugared fruit slide down his throat. Slippery and wonderfully cool. He wolfed down another piece.

She sat quietly against the rail and hugged her knees to her chest. He cut a guarded look her way. Hair dark as a raven's wing swirled in unruly ringlets around a high-cheekboned face. Large, curious eyes stared back at him, bold and unafraid. A faded bruise along her jawline added to her rough look. Wonder how she got that? And what did she mean about haints? He swallowed hard.

"What was that back there? The drums, fire, and all?"

"Reckon it be some kind of Voodoo, Come-to-Jesus meeting."

"Jesus? You're telling me that...that thing in the lightning was Jesus?"

"Their Jesus.

"Why'd you stop me from getting closer?"

"Because you don't believe."

Her sharp comeback shocked him.

"You busting up their sacred ritual would be like kicking down the church door in the middle of the Lord's

Prayer. Nobody would take kindly to that."

How'd she know he was a non-believer? "You're mighty quick to defend them so."

"They ain't hurtin' no one, Benjamin. Besides, the way I see it, their jumping and cavorting around with snakes ain't much different than the talking-in-tongues, rolling-on-the-floor going ons what happens at one of Jedidiah's saving-of-the-soul gatherings."

Peach can empty, he leaned back and closed his eyes. Felt older than dirt, but she was right. The sweet fruit got his blood to pumping again. Eyes opened and he sighed.

"Might interest you to know that Wayne's telling everyone who'll listen that these people stole you away. That one of them even turned into a jaguar and damn near ripped his ear off."

He threw that last part in on purpose to test her reaction. Most people would've gasped at the mention of a man-eating jungle cat slinking around, but only a slight lift of her chin betrayed her casual answer.

"That so?"

"Yeah. That's why I'm here. I'm hunting for the both of you."

She giggled. "The way you stomp and clomp through these wilds? Anything with a lick of sense would've high-tailed it long before you'd even seen tracks. Shoot, if I hadn't sent that crow to lead you to the spring, you'd still be chasing your tail panting for water."

He gawked at her. She sent the crow? Bullshit. Nothing added up with this girl. On one hand, she acted more grown-up and confident than a lot of adults he'd been around. There was a practical down-to-earth quality about her he liked. Her playful teasing tone surprised him, but made him smile just the same. In a lot of ways, she reminded him of Danni.

But on the other hand, a breath of untamed air and downright mystery circled her as well. Even though a gentle wisdom lived in those violet eyes, their smoldering witchy look unnerved him.

"You're wasting your time, Benjamin. There be no jaguar in these swamps. Jedidiah Wayne is a liar. That ain't what happened that night."

He scooted closer. "Suppose you tell me what did."

Seconds melted into minutes, and no answer came. He'd get to the truth even if he had to wait all night in this smelly God-forsaken alligator pit to get it. The tapping of his boot on the wood step echoed out into blackness. Long fingers drummed a mindless rhythm on the porch rail. He studied the two-room shack and shook his head. How did she live in a place that smelled like dirty laundry, mud, and rotting garbage? Right before giving in and asking her again, she sighed. Her voice came low but packed a fierce punch.

"Mama got sick and died. That's what happened."

The wind flew from his gut. He fumbled for words.

"I…I'm…Wayne never said anything about his wife being dead."

"That don't surprise me none."

He didn't want to pry. Hated to ask more questions. It was impossible to look into a heart, but he felt the pain that lived there. He knew firsthand how long it took for the scar of losing a loved one to heal. How much it hurt when people kept picking at the scab, but he had to know.

"Had she been sick long?"

"No." Her face screwed into a frown. "That's the

funny part."

Slender legs uncurled. She stood and wrapped her arm around a weathered post. Puzzled, he watched her search the night for answers that weren't there.

"Mama never had a puny bone in her body. One day she was hauling water and choppin' wood like always. The next day she took sick. The day after that she died."

Two steps put him close enough to feel her warmth. "What happened then?"

Her back stiffened.

Every nerve in his body wanted to reach out to her, but he hesitated. Better go easy. Hand on her arm he turned her to him. A gentle finger under the chin tilted her face up to meet his.

"That bruise on your cheek some of Wayne's handiwork?"

Anger flashed in deep eyes. "He came after me. I got away. Ran to the swamp. And that's all there be to it."

He knew that wasn't all. "And his face?"

"A jaguar clawed him."

Tension crackled between them. Sweat popped on his brow. Hers was bone dry.

"Thought you said there wasn't any such animal here."

"There ain't. Not tonight anyway."

His jaw clenched so hard his teeth ached. The slight grin that pulled at her lips irked him.

"You need to come into town with me. Tell the sheriff your story. You don't have to be scared of Wayne. I'll…the law will protect you. You don't need to hide out in this hell-hole anymore."

"One man's hell can be another one's paradise."

"Are you serious? Look at this rat trap. It's only got

two rooms, for Christ's sakes."

"Well, just how many rooms does a person need, Benjamin?"

"Hell, you don't even have electricity or running water."

"Ya don't miss what ya never had."

He ran his hand through his hair. Stubborn to the bone. "Nothing I can say or do will get you to leave here, will it?"

"Ain't likely."

She placed a gentle hand on his wrist. "I belong here, Benjamin. It's mighty kind of you to fret, but I ain't a'feared of no man, especially Jedidiah Wayne...but you should be."

A chill shot up his spine. "What's that supposed to mean?"

Maybe he imagined it. Maybe the effects of a long day in the heat and sun coupled with a hungry gut, a tired butt and a short night of drums pounding his head had scrambled his thinking. He didn't know. But stagnant, humid air cooled and whispered to the tree tops. Night sounds of swamp creatures hushed as if the crickets and bullfrogs were holding their breath. A shimmering much like moonbeams on still water, danced just out of reach. He blinked, not trusting what he saw. And the girl in front of him stood taller and spoke with a dangerous, powerful voice that made the hairs on the back of his neck stand at attention.

"Jedidiah Wayne runs with the devil. He preys on the innocent. He means to destroy them."

Voice barely above a whisper, he asked, "How do you know that?"

"I seen it."

"The haints…ghosts show you?"

"Their souls cry out to me, Benjamin. But I ain't the only one they seek."

"Me?"

Dark eyes turned to granite. He shivered.

"Jedidiah will come for you, too."

That did it. He tore loose from her grip and took a deep gulp of stagnant air.

"Let him. I got a bullet with his name on it."

"Evil can twist and turn and slip through cracks, Benjamin, and never plays fair. Voodoo drums turned you plumb stupid tonight, and their sound ain't nothing compared to the forces of the wicked. Guns can't kill something what lives in shadow and moves like smoke. Ain't the first time you been told this. You best be listening."

Lady Tibatha. Christ's sakes. How did she know about her?

"I just do."

"Don't!" He paced back and forth, swearing with each step. "Don't answer my questions before I ask them, damn it."

He stood in front of her and jabbed a finger at her chest. "Just stay out of my head, ok?"

"I ain't gonna promise ya that. Come on. I'll take you back."

"What?"

"Don't think you want to spend the night here."

"You think right, but it's black as pitch, and you have no idea where my jeep is." Course neither did he, but she didn't know that. The twinkle in her eye and the giggle in her voice told him different.

"Ain't no problem for me to see in the dark." She

picked up the lantern. "But you can carry a light. Take a hold of my hand."

Once again he dogged her footsteps. Trees, twisted and distorted, loomed giant-size in the lantern's yellow beam. Spooky how they swayed in the breeze. Back and forth. He heard their whispering. Felt them breathe. In and out. Knot holes became all-seeing eyes. Branches transformed into bent arms with long brittle fingers stretching out to grab a piece of him. A grayish-white blanket of mist rose from the spongy ground. An owl let out a screech that would either wake the dead or kill the living.

God, he hated this place. Hated not knowing what prowled in the darkness. Hated the constant feeling of uneasiness, how scrambled his thoughts became and the jitters in the pit of his stomach.

One Christmas, Danni had given him a snow globe. Fascinated, he'd turn the glass orb over and over and watch snow swirl around people forever trapped under the glass dome, their lives controlled by some outside force.

Frustration welled inside him. He felt like those snow-globe people. A spell covered this swamp like an umbrella, a magic curse that rendered him useless. He'd be lost as a Sunday school kid on a snipe hunt if she let go of his hand.

Usually the one in control, he found himself tied to a girl twenty years younger who knew his thoughts before he did. A girl with the teasing innocence of a child and wisdom older than her years. A girl with the crescent moon in her eyes, and the strength of a jungle cat lurking inside her.

The dark hulk of the jeep made him sigh in relief.

He climbed into the seat and put the lantern beside him. Thank God he'd left the keys in the ignition. One turn. The mechanical sound of the engine roaring to life broke the hex and jolted him back into the real world. In less than an hour he'd be home where everything made sense and where he could kiss this night goodbye once and for all.

"Bethany Ann, I don't understand much of what went on here tonight. But I'm glad I found you."

"You didn't find me. I found you, remember? And the next time you come here, bring a canteen."

He rolled his eyes and shifted into reverse. "No offense, but there isn't going to be a next time. I'm never gonna step foot in this muggy, stinking, Voodoo playground ever again."

Her impish grin and cocked eyebrow froze his breath. What did she know that he didn't?

"Never say never, Benjamin. It has a way of biting you in the butt."

She reached in and dropped something beside him. "Hanna. Hanna Miller will be the first he'll come for." She pointed at the seat. "And that belongs around your neck. Not under the bed."

Heart pounding, hands shaking he gawked at the red *gris-gris* bag lying beside him. Dumbfounded, insides quivering like jelly, he jerked his head up. "Bethany Ann?" He swallowed the lump in his throat. "How the hell…?"

Too late.

She'd become one with the shadows and slipped into darkness.

Chapter 18

"Well it's about time. I was getting ready to call out the hounds."

Ben scowled. It had been well after midnight when he'd dropped into bed. Dreams of snakes and live-roasted chickens tormented his sleep. Dog tired, he was in no mood for anyone this morning, especially Sheriff Tate with his good, ol' boy mannerisms and jargon.

"Just doing what you told me. I was in the swamps."

"Figured that. Thought you'd be back before sundown though."

He twirled the straight-back chair around, sank into the hard seat, and shut his eyes. Lord, God, he'd sell his soul for just a whiff of steaming hot coffee. "I got…delayed."

Buford reached under the desk and produced a thermos. The scent of chicory forced Ben to open one eye. Buford pushed a cup across the table. Ok. Maybe Tate's backwoods mindset wasn't all that bad.

"Rough night?"

"You don't know the half of it." He took a couple of sips of the strong brew and sighed. Nothing better in the morning than a cup of Community Coffee. "Let's just say I understand your reluctance to step foot in that place."

"Find any jaguars?"

"Nope." Another swallow. "But I did find the girl."

"Wayne's daughter?"

He chuckled. "Bethany Ann will be the first to tell you that she's no relation to Jedidiah Wayne."

"Well now, that's mighty interesting."

"Yep. Says he's pure evil. Hates the ground he walks on."

"Bethany Ann?" Buford scratched his chin. "Don't recall Wayne ever mentioning her name before."

"Yeah, and that reminds me." Benjamin straightened in his chair and slid the empty cup back to be topped off. "You told me she was a kid. I expected to find some gawky, long-legged, stringy-haired, half-wit teenager. What I found was just the opposite. Oh, she's rough around the edges for sure, but Bethany Ann is no kid."

Buford's right eyebrow arched. "Ya don't say."

"Don't give me that look. I'm just stating facts." He retrieved the mug and blew across the rim. "She's a bushel of contradictions mixed together into one little stick of TNT. Shy one minute, teasing the next. Naïve and savvy all at the same time."

Then, of course, there was her other side. That mystifying bewitching side that gave him the willies, but Buford didn't need to know that.

"She could burn your soul in half with those violet eyes of hers."

Buford grinned. "Them are some facts."

"Yeah, well, there's more. We had it figured right. Wayne did come after her that night. Slapped her around pretty good from the looks of the bruise on her cheek."

"Damn bastard. He harm her in any other way?"

"You mean rape?"

"That's exactly what I mean."

Ben shook his head and gulped down the last bit of coffee. "No. She got away and ran to the swamp to hide out. But get this, she said her mother died that night."

"What?" Buford flopped back into the office chair. Cracked leather groaned, and the front legs reared off the floor. "Damn, I hate hearing that. I didn't know Rachel Wayne all that well. She kept to herself, mostly. But folks said she had a heart of gold."

"Don't you think it strange that Wayne didn't mention his wife died on the exact same night his daughter was kidnapped and he was attacked?"

"Yep. Mighty peculiar all right." He leaned forward. The chair settled back into place. "In fact, this whole case stinks to high heaven. I got a couple of daughters myself. If someone had stolen and hid one of my girls in the swamp, I'd burn down every square foot looking for her. Either that or I'd be camped out on the sheriff's doorstep until he found her. But I ain't seen hide nor hair of Wayne since he first reported this whole mess. Maybe it's high time we paid him a visit."

Buford opened the bottom desk drawer and pulled out his .45 automatic. Ben stared in disbelief. He'd never seen a pistol strapped around Buford's wide waist, ever.

"Hey, boss, you expecting trouble?"

"Nope. Just believe in covering all the bases."

When he reached back into the drawer and pulled out a red bag, Ben about fell on the floor.

"Close your mouth, son, before your tongue falls out."

"You?" Ben sputtered. "You carry a *gris-gris* bag?"

"Ben, I'm gonna let you in on a little secret. Half the boys on the New Orleans PD wear these around their necks, right beside their Saint Michael medals.

"Yeah, but Saint Michael is the patron saint of policemen, and he's ——"

"Christian?"

"You know I didn't mean it like that. It's just well, I didn't picture you for the Voodoo type."

"Voodoo ain't got nothing to do with it." Buford threw a wink. "Like I said, just covering all the bases, that's all."

"Boss." Ben chuckled and stood up. "I'm beginning to think there's more to you than what meets the eye. What are you planning on telling Wayne?"

Buford let out a hee-haw that shook the walls. "Son, I ain't gonna tell that son-of-a-bitch nothing. You are. I'm just going along to watch the show."

Ben knew Buford's 1950 White Rose Ford was the sheriff's pride and joy, and he made sure to wipe his feet before he slid into the seat next to his beefy boss.

"It ain't Sunday, so we'll stop by Wayne's place first," Buford said. "If he ain't there, we'll mosey on over to the church."

Ben opened his mouth to reply, but the words froze in his throat when Buford's size twelve tromped the gas pedal. The speedometer was hitting fifty when they passed Dixon's Feed Store at the edge of town. "Sure you don't want to turn the lights and si-reen on?" Ben asked.

"Don't see no reason to."

Ben smiled to himself. He'd been teasing. Buford might be slow and methodical in the office but when behind the wheel, he turned into a regular speed demon. Just another thing about the man he didn't know. Wonder what else he'd learn before the day was over?

Ten miles out of town they turned east and went five

more on a dirt road that was little more than a cow path. Air turned muggy and the garbage-dump scent that wafted in through the car window told Ben they were driving on the lip of the swamp. Buford slowed and cleared his throat.

"Ben, there's some things you need to know before we get any closer. Wayne and the others who live out this way are dyed-in-the-wool, back-wood country folk who don't take kindly to strangers, especially the law. We're going to be about as welcome as a darkie at a Klan meeting. They're a close-knit bunch who think Jedidiah Wayne is both the Father and the Son and Robert E Lee is the Holy Ghost. They tolerate me cause I was born and raised here, but you've got three strikes against ya, going in."

He counted down on fat fingers.

"One. You're not from around these parts.

"Two. You're well educated.

"Three. You wear a badge.

"Tread light. Be polite. It's best to just smile and keep your opinions to yourself no matter how difficult that may be. Think you can handle that?"

Ben nodded. "Yes, sir."

Two blue-tick hounds and a chewed-on pit bull came howling down the road like a tribe of wild Comanches on the warpath.

"Here there! Get on now," Buford yelled and waved his arm out the window. "Back off, ya hear."

He pointed to his right and his voice fell back into the jovial, county boy tone that Ben was accustomed to. "Well, we're about ready to find out if you can or not. Yonder there is the

Wayne place."

The two-story farmhouse surprised Ben. He'd expected to find a run-down shack with cows in the garden, chickens in the outhouse, and pigs wallowing in a muddy front yard. The house could use a new coat of paint, and the porch that surrounded it needed shoring up here and there, but for the most part, everything was in pretty good shape. Trees threw shade across a weeded garden and sheets penned to the clothesline out back waved lazily in the hot breeze.

"Nicer than what I expected," he told Buford.

"The property mirrors the owner. All of this belongs to Hester Wayne, Jedidiah's sister.

She's firm about 'a place for everything and everything in its place.' Can't stand the woman."

"Why's that?"

Buford snorted. "Hester Wayne is the meanest, most hateful strip of dried up beef jerky you'll ever meet. She'd just as soon spit in your eye as look at ya." Buford pulled up in front of the house and switched the car off. He gazed over at Ben and winked. "Just follow my lead."

He walked up the porch steps and stood off to the side waiting for someone to answer the sheriff's knock. The pit bull with the gnawed-on ear hiked his leg on the Ford's rear tire. He heard Buford's muffled, "damn mangy mutt," a few seconds before the creak of the screen door. Buford tipped his hat.

"Mornin', Miss Hester."

A dry, raspy voice set Ben's nerves on edge.

"Sheriff Tate. What business brings you here?"

Buford grabbed him by the shirt and pulled him forward. "Miss Hester, this here is my new deputy, Benjamin Sol. He's got some news about Bethany Ann. I wonder if we might speak to Mrs. Rachael?"

Hester's beady dark eyes darted from his face to Buford's. Reminded him of the way Bethany Ann's crow had studied him that day in the swamp. The crow had more personality.

"Sister Rachael passed a few weeks back."

"Oh, I'm so sorry," Buford said and removed his hat. "I hadn't heard. Well, bless her heart. What happened?"

Ben bit the inside of his mouth to hide the smirk. Not only was Buford a speed driver but a damn good actor as well.

"I look like a doctor to you? Took sick and died. All's I know."

"Well, I'm mighty sorry I missed the funeral. Rachel Ellen was a good woman."

"Private service. Just family."

Not one blink. The woman's heart must be made of stone.

Buford clicked his tongue and shook his head. "Well, it's a shame, a crying shame. Is Jedidiah at home then?"

"He's down by the water. Baptizing."

Ben couldn't stop himself. "Baptizing? On a Thursday? Thought that was only done on Sundays."

Whoo-eee, the look she shot him would've curdled milk.

"For your information, Deputy Sol, the Lord God Almighty doesn't have a watch in His pocket or a calendar on His wall. When it's time to save a soul, He knows."

She turned back to the sheriff. "Is that all you needin'? I got chores."

Buford settled his Stetson back on his head. "Yes,

ma'am. We'll just be heading on down to the river. Thank ya' kindly."

They weren't two steps off the porch before the slam of the door shouted behind them.

Buford turned the car around and started down the narrow lane. When they were out of sight from the house, he stopped. "You notice that big tree a few yards off from the barn?"

"You mean the one with the freshly dug grave under it?"

"Yep, that'd be the one."

Chapter 19

Ben glanced over at the sheriff.

Buford let out a long breath. "Didn't even have the common decency to bury the woman with her own kin. She's all by herself out there under that magnolia. Hell of a way to spend eternity." He shook his head. "Yes sir, it's a crying shame."

The sheriff was right. It *was* a damn shame, but not for Rachel. She was dead and gone. Maybe in a better place. Ben didn't know. It was Bethany Ann that was all alone. He doubted she even knew where her mother had been laid to rest. She'd never be able to leave flowers on her own mama's grave, especially as long as Hester Wayne ruled the roost.

Hester.

Lord in heaven. What a piece of work that woman was. If sour pickles had crinkly skin and could walk, they'd be called Hesters, instead of Dills. Even if Wayne hadn't tried to rape her, he'd bet a month's pay Bethany Ann would've still run away. Living in the swamps would be a picnic compared to life with Aunt Hester.

"Ben, you ever witness an honest-to goodness-old-time-washed-in-the-water river baptism?"

"No, sir."

"Well, it's a powerful sight. Folks around here take it mighty serious. Now, I know you ain't a very religious fella, and that's okay by me. I don't understand it, but everyone has right to their own beliefs. But, for my sake, try to refrain from blurting out anything that could cause any trouble."

Ben grinned. "You mean like questioning the whole, 'born again' thing?"

He laughed at Buford's oversized groan. "I'm just joking, boss. I promise. I'll be good."

They found the site without any trouble and pulled alongside the other cars and pickups parked in the tall grass. Even a few wagons with horses rested under big shade trees. Buford eased the Ford's door shut. The slamming of a car door would be downright rude and disrespectful to the sound of gospel singing that floated on the soft breeze. They walked up behind the group of folks gathered at the water's edge. He had to admit, it was an inspiring sight.

Women in simple dresses of light grey and blue surrounded the riverbank, their skirts waving like cotton wildflowers in the easy wind. Trees of leafy green stood out bold against a cloudless blue sky. Men, some dressed in their Sunday best and others in faded overalls, stood by their womenfolk with calloused hands raised in praise. The river flowed with a lazy current so peaceful the chirping of birds blended with the singing and could be heard all around. Ben took a deep breath, heavy with the scent of honeysuckle, water, and wood. Twenty voices joined as one, and the soulful melody of the hymn rang out crystal clear.

"Oh brothers, let's go down. Let's go down. Oh, brothers, let's go down to the river to pray."

He knew that song. A lifetime ago, it'd been one of his favorites. Religious or not, hearing the words sung in pure harmony surrounded in nature's beauty had an uplifting, soothing quality about it. Almost made him want to believe again—almost.

Ben stepped closer, and there, in all his glory, stood Jedidiah Wayne. His back was turned, but dressed in gray and blue with his hair oiled slick, there was no mistaking the Reverend.

Huh. Ben had him pictured broader across the shoulders and bigger boned, but just as tall. He stood in waist-high water, a snip of a girl by his side. Long blonde curls falling to her waist, dressed in what looked like a man's white undershirt, she didn't look any older than twelve or thirteen. Ben could see her thin shoulders tremble. Wayne, however, had a firm, close hold on her. A little too close to Ben's way of thinking.

Wayne raised one arm high toward heaven pulling the girl even tighter against his side. His voice, too dramatic and overpowering in the tranquility of the river, destroyed any momentary contentment Ben had felt.

"Brothers. Sisters. We are gathered here today to witness the power and the glory of the Holy Spirit. Brother John Wesley has requested that this heavenly lamb of God be washed whole in the water, to be cleansed and forgiven of all sins."

"Amen, Brother Jed, Amen! Praise God!"

Inside Ben snorted. How many sins could a twelve-year-old have committed?

Wayne gazed down at the girl. "Tell me, beautiful child, are you ready to receive? To be filled with the Spirit? To make a union with our Lord and Savior, Jesus Christ?"

A voice so tiny Ben strained to hear, whispered a weak, "I am, sir."

The wind kicked up and stirred the current. A chill

raced up Ben's spine. Wayne placed a hand on the girl's forehead, the other in the small of her back and laid her backwards into the muddy water.

"I baptize you in the name of the Father."

He lifted the shaking girl up only to lay her backwards again. On the sly, his hand slipped under the garment. Ben tensed, doubting what he'd seen.

"And the Son."

Up.

Back.

His hand moved farther.

"And in the Holy Ghost."

Ben gritted his teeth. Bold move to grab a kid like that in public. What must that girl be thinking under the heavy darkness of the water, completely at the mercy of a man she thought holy, whose hand groped and fondled? What was the matter with these people? Were they really that blind? He shot a glance at the sheriff. Buford's clenched jaw confirmed that he hadn't imagined what he'd just seen.

Shouts of "hallelujah, hallelujah," ricocheted off stone and wood.

Maybe they hadn't seen. More likely they had. What was this strange hold Wayne had on them? They acted more like a cult than a congregation. Perhaps Bethany Ann had been right. Maybe Wayne was in cahoots with the devil.

Wayne helped the girl to shore, the cotton shirt clinging to her small body, molded to every curve and line. A man, who Ben guessed was Brother John Wesley, waded in and reached for her.

Ben bit his lip. Christ sakes. Someone hurry and throw a coat around the kid.

A woman stepped forward and answered Ben's wish. She wrapped the girl in a patchwork quilt and hugged the cloaked figure to her side.

A chorus of, "Shall We Gather at the River" broke out. Walking back to their cars, they passed within a couple of feet of where Ben stood. The girl, long wet hair plastered to a chalk-white face, shook like a trapped fawn. She raised her gaze from the ground to lock with his. Large green eyes, scared and confused, tugged at his heart and lit the fuse on his anger.

This was blasphemy.

Saving one's soul was sacred. Once upon a time, he'd even believed that. These good folks still did. This reverent ceremony had been tainted by the actions of the very man they placed their trust in. A man of God should be good. Honorable. Humble. But Jedidiah Wayne was none of these. Dirty, lecherous, and deceiving was more like it. A hypocrite who made a mockery out of the religion he so vehemently preached.

It made Ben want to puke. And folks wondered why he'd lost his faith?

"Ben, stay here. I'll go talk to Wayne."

"Don't try and stop me, Buford. I got a few things I want to say to that bastard."

"Ben."

"Sorry, boss. Gotta break that promise."

The sheriff hurried forward and put his bulky frame between Ben and the preacher. "Ah, excuse me, Reverend." He removed his hat. "But I have news about your daughter."

Jedidiah turned.

Ben gasped. He stood frozen in the glare of Wayne's cold stare.

The preacher's voice thundered.

"Glory be to God! We are indeed blessed today, brothers and sisters for the Lord has sent this man into our flock to be filled with the Holy Ghost." Before Ben could slap it away, Wayne placed a firm hand on his right shoulder and squeezed hard.

The reverend bowed his head and closed his eyes acting deep in prayer. He took in a huge breath, raised his head and left arm toward the sky. "Witness the power of the Lord." Eyes opened, and his hand came crashing down to grab Ben's opposite shoulder.

"The Spirit of the Lord is upon you. Go, and know ye have been born again!"

Speechless, Ben watched Wayne strut away shouting out hallelujahs and amens at the top of his lungs. Stark raving mad, Ben thought. The lunatic thinks he's Jesus.

Buford's hand on his arm made him jump.

"Ben, you want to tell me just what happened here?"

He stared at Buford for a heartbeat before his temper exploded.

"Spirit of the Lord, my ass!"

A possum grin spread across the sheriff's face. "That's more like it. Didn't think you'd been touched. Have to admit, though, you had me going for a minute what with acting so dumbfounded. What was that all about anyway?"

"His face surprised me, that's all."

"Oh, you mean with that ugly scar and all?"

"No. I mean I recognized him."

He took a deep breath. "Buford, listen to me and listen good. That man isn't any more a preacher than you are. And his name isn't Jedidiah Wayne."

96

"It ain't? Then what the hell is it?

"Lucius Stone."

"Ain't never heard of him. Who is he?"

"He's a child molester and a murderer. And I've been hunting him for over ten years so I could put a bullet right between his beady eyes."

Chapter 20

From a half mile away, I felt him step into the swamp.

Restlessness always walked side-by-side with Benjamin, but more so today, and heaviness surrounded his heart. I settled down on the steps to wait. He wouldn't have no trouble finding me today.

He walked out from the wilds, a canteen strapped to his waist and a knapsack on his back. I smiled. "Hey, Benjamin."

A hangdog grin made him cuter than a little bug's ear.

"Ok, you were right. Never say never."

"What's in the bag?"

He walked up the steps and into the cabin. "Some stuff for you."

My heart jumped as high as me off the porch steps. "Presents? For me?"

"Don't get so excited. It isn't much, just a few things I thought you'd need."

Didn't matter, I couldn't wait to tear into that backpack.

Canned goods were first. Then candles, matches, and kerosene for the lamps. Some fishing hooks came next. The bars of soap and toothpaste made me grin. "What's this?" I asked.

"An Army cot. It's easy to put together. Granted, it

isn't a four-poster bed with a goose-down mattress, but it sure beats sleeping on the hard floor."

I dropped my hands and stepped back. A confused look crossed his face.

"What's wrong? You act like you've never been given anything before."

"I haven't."

My voice was a whisper. Didn't mean for it to come out that soft, just did.

"Only presents I ever got was a few small things from Mama at Christmas and my birthday. Jedidiah didn't hold to gift-giving, said it was wasteful, but Mama always found a way to sneak me something." I pointed at the table. "These here things are more than I ever got in my whole life."

For a heartbeat, he just stared, then that little boy's smile of his lit up his face. He reached back inside the pack. "Well then, you're gonna love this."

He put six bottles on the table. Curious, I walked over and picked up one full of purple liquid.

"What is it?"

"Nehi Grape soda, otherwise known as the nectar of the gods."

Didn't mean nothing to me.

He backed up and frowned. "Don't tell me you've never heard of soda pop?"

"Well, I mostly certainly have. I ain't no country bumpkin, ya know. One hot summer day, Mama, Sarah Rose and me split a bottle of RC Cola at Baker's Emporium. I just didn't know it came in colors, that's all."

I don't know why that tickled him so much, but it was good to hear his laugh and see his eyes sparkle 'cause I knew Benjamin found very little in life to laugh about.

He reached into his pocket and pulled out a bottle opener. Pop. Fizz. He handed me a bottle. I took a swig.

"Lord Almighty, Benjamin. This beats the sap out of RC Cola."

"It's even better when ice cold."

Maybe so, but it tasted mighty good warm.

"Benjamin, this is just like Christmas, only in July, and I'm touched by your kindness. But I know something powerful is gnawing on ya. You want to tell me the real reason you came here?"

The light in his eyes dulled, and made me sad I'd spoiled the moment. He shook his head.

"When I was training to become a lawman, I was told my best asset was my gut. I can size up a situation or a man within seconds. But for the life of me, I can't figure you out. You're a puzzle, Bethany Ann. A young, very pretty jigsaw puzzle."

Nobody ever talked to me like that. "What does that mean?" I asked.

"Well, first, there's your outside pieces, the border. You're age, hair, face, all the physical things. That's easy to put together. It's the inside pieces that are hard to connect.

"There are pieces of a typical teenage girl who gets excited over presents and grape soda, who is shy and blushes when called pretty."

I felt heat creep up my neck, and I ducked my head.

"Then there are the parts that find wonder in things that others think useless. This swamp, for example. I hate this place. Where I see sticks and muddy water, you see green, lush bushes that give shade to the critters you love so much. I see butt-ugly, man eating alligators while you praise their scaly hides."

"That's on account they be the spirit of the swamps."

"What the hell does that mean?"

"They be dangerous, wild and wooly for certain, just like the swamps. But they serve a purpose too. Just like the wilds. The wetlands is home to hundreds of birds, wildlife, trees, flowers, and ferns. Them gators protect all that. They be guardians of a sort, prowling the water and land, watching over what flies, slithers, and crawls here from those who would do harm, trespass again' it."

"That's just what I mean. Some parts of you are young and innocent. While other sides are older than the hills and wiser than Solomon."

He paused and took a drink. I laughed at his purple lips.

"But then there are those damn mysterious pieces. The ones you keep hidden in the box. You talk to ghosts and see em' too. Read folks' minds. See the future." He stared at me. "I call those the black pieces, not because they're bad, but because I can't figure them out."

"Only the wicked need to fear those, Benjamin."

"That kind of talk chills my blood. You look different when you say those things. Your eyes get darker, your voice turns deeper, and your face changes from an innocent girl into a...a...sorceress or a witch." He paused. "Or even a ferocious jungle cat."

Didn't surprise me none that he knew I could change into a panther, but for him to say the words out loud did.

He drained the rest of his bottle. "You needed the things I brought today, but they're also a bribe. I have to ask you a huge favor. A favor that means you'll have to take those dark pieces out of the box."

"What is it?"

"I need you to talk to someone who's dead."

Never saw that coming. The look on my face musta' been a funny sight because he laughed, opened another pop, and slid it across the table. I took a deep gulp.

"But I need to tell you some things first. Things about my past." He tugged at his shirt collar. "It's too stuffy in here, let's go outside."

A faint scent of possible rain surprised me when we stepped outside. A slight breeze stirred the tree tops. Birds chirped and the katydids hummed. I sat with my back leaned against the cabin's wall. He sat opposite of me. I could feel his innards twisting and turning.

"I didn't know my real dad. Mom never talked about him. Didn't matter to me, she was all I needed. But I guess she got tired of struggling to raise a son all by herself, so she hooked up with a man, a widower, and got married. Made me mad, not because I got a stepfather, but because he had a daughter. I wanted a brother."

He smiled but there weren't any happiness behind it.

"Her name was Danielle. She was a few years older than me, and knew I was disappointed in not having a brother to play with, so one day she said, 'Tell ya what. Why don't you call me Danni. Will that make ya feel better?' From that day on, Danni was my best friend. She took me under her wing and helped me make friends at school. Summertime she even took me fishing and swimming at this secret spot in the woods behind our house."

I saw tears in his eyes, and they sparked the ones in mine. Maybe I was a puzzle with lots of pieces, but there were many sides to Benjamin as well. Sides he kept hidden, same as me.

"For the most part, everything was good even though I couldn't stand my stepfather. He was rude and crude, couldn't figure out what Mom saw in him, but she seemed happy and he left me alone. Mom worked nights, so I pretty well just did as I pleased. I noticed that some days Danni acted strange. She'd run off to the woods to be by herself. I asked Mom about it. She said that sometimes girls just needed alone time."

He raised an eyebrow. "Is that true?"

Never thought about it. I shrugged.

"Then Mom got sick. I prayed on my knees every night for God to make her better. But. He didn't. She died."

"Like mine."

"Exactly like yours."

So this was what tied me to Benjamin. I could never figure out the bond before. Strange both our mamas passing that way.

"I couldn't handle her being gone. Felt lost. On a dare, I lied about my age and joined the Army. They weren't supposed to take me. But I was big and tall, the war was heating up, and they needed men. They never bothered to check my age. When they told me I was going overseas, I sent a telegram home to let Danni know. A week later, I got a letter from her. That letter changed my life, but not for the good."

His voice broke. I waited. Didn't think he was going to say anymore, but directly he sighed and started again.

"Danni wrote she'd been living with a secret. An awful secret. For years her daddy, my stepfather had been…uh ….."

"Ruining her."

His head jerked up. "How did you know that?"

"Just did."

"Nobody knew. Mom never suspected anything wrong. I was in my own world. He'd come to her room in the middle of the night. Sometimes he'd grab her in the barn when Mom and I weren't around. He told her if she dared tell anyone, he'd kill me."

On wash day I'd watch Mama grab one end of a shirt and twist the cloth tight to wring out all the water. The sadness that filled Benjamin to the brim reminded me of that sight. Felt like strong hands was wringing all the blood out of his heart and mine.

"She was going to have a baby."

"Her own daddy's child?"

He didn't answer, just nodded.

I couldn't think of one thing to say. But the sadness that only minutes before had made my heart ache turned to anger. Full-out, seeing red anger.

"Danni didn't know what to do. She had no one to turn to. Said she couldn't bring a child into the world that way. She couldn't face the shame and humiliation. Said she prayed on it and had made her decision, that she loved me and to stay safe.

"Bethany Ann, those words scared the hell out of me. I got an emergency leave from the Red Cross and rushed home, but I couldn't find her or my stepfather. Folks said he'd gone to live with family, but they couldn't remember where. Mississippi, Arkansas maybe Louisiana. They weren't sure. When I asked where Danni was, they said they assumed she went with him. But she hadn't. Her clothes were still in the house."

He scrambled to his feet and paced the porch. I scooted back into a corner, made myself small to get out of his way.

"I searched all over and couldn't find her, and then it dawned on me. I ran to the woods, to the old swimming hole. That's where I found her."

Three steps one way, three another. Back and forth, Benjamin worked himself into a lather.

"I prayed, Bethany Ann. Prayed hard that she was just resting against that old tree. But God refused to hear my prayers yet again. She'd killed herself. Slit her wrists with a razor blade."

He turned and threw words.

"Her own father killed her. Maybe he didn't pull that blade across her thin veins, but he was the reason. I vowed over her lifeless body that no matter how long it took, I'd track him down and bring him to justice. But I had to go fight half of Germany before I could even start looking. I'd almost given up hope of finding him—until now."

"You found him here?"

"Yeah, I found him, all right. The sorry bastard changed his name."

He stopped dead in his tracks and looked me square in the eye.

"Jedidiah Wayne is my stepfather."

Chapter 21

"Are you shittin' me?

Benjamin's eyebrows shot up. The way he looked reminded me so much of how Sarah Rose reacted after one of my swearing rants, I almost laughed. A weak smile tried to pull up the corners of his mouth.

"Nope. I saw him yesterday morning. Even with that big scar across his face, I recognized him right off."

"Did he know you?"

Wore-out from walking a mile on my front porch, he sat on the steps and leaned his back against the railing.

"Can't say for sure. If he did, he covered it up by taking me by the shoulders and making a big show of bringing down the Holy Ghost into my soul."

Stunned. I was downright stunned. "You let him lay hands on you?"

"He's insane, Bethany Ann, and sly. Sly like a fox. Got folks thinking he's God's right-hand man."

"He put his mark on you, Benjamin. You best beware."

He snorted.

"Don't laugh at things you don't understand."

"Don't make him out to be more than what he is, Bethany Ann."

"And just who do you think he is, *Benjamin?*"

"He's a deranged, egotistical, demented man, Bethany Ann. But that's all he is, just a man. Not the devil and certainly not the second coming."

"Oh, ouch, bet all them big words you just pulled out of your ass, hurt real bad."

He almost fell off the steps laughing so hard.

His laughter sounded so good ringing out through the trees and water. Birds fell quiet like they was listening close to the strange yet happy sound. Lightning flashed in the distance and the fresh smell of threatening rain got stronger. He looked over at me and sighed.

"In war you try not to make friends. Chances are the minute you do, your buddy ends up dead. But it's hard not to reach out to someone. My buddy was Josh Tremble. We were different as night and day. He was a fast-talking Yankee from Boston, and I was a slow-drawling rebel boy from Chattanooga. Like trying to mix oil and water, but for some reason, we just clicked."

I thought of Sarah Rose and smiled.

After basic training, Josh went to train as a medic. He and I went separate ways, but we stayed in touch. After the war, he became a doctor, and I pinned on a star. We joined up one weekend to celebrate living. We got drunk and spilled out guts about our hopes, dreams and fears. I broke down and told him everything about Danni." He took a deep breath.

"Josh told me that people didn't talk much about men like Lucius…Jedidiah even in the medical profession. In fact, if he hadn't been half-in-the-bag, I doubt he would've said anything more about it to me.

"He went on to say that no one wants to admit that Uncle Harry or dear ol' gramps dreams about doing unnatural things to children. They'd rather sweep it under the rug and pretend it never happens. But it does, more than what people think. He said those kinds of men have a sickness, and they can't help what they do. They don't know it's wrong. In fact, a lot of them love the children and think they're helping them."

Love? I did a slow burn. What Jedidiah did to Sarah Rose and tried to do to me had nothing to do with love.

"Benjamin, I ain't no doctor, and I may not understand them fifty-cent words you've been throwing around, but I know bullshit when I step in it. If they don't know what they're doing is wrong, then why do they sneak around in the dead of night doing it? If they don't know it's wrong, why do they scare the beejesus out innocent young'uns, making them stay quiet with threats of hellfire and eternal damnation or with killing their loved ones?

"And another thing. When Jedidiah slapped me down on that bed, pinned my arms over my head, and shoved his way between my legs, I guaran-damn-tee tell you, it weren't love shining in his eyes. Them kinds of folks are pure evil. Don't tell me they don't know what they're doing ain't wrong. That dog just don't hunt, Benjamin."

Memories of the night Jedidiah slobbered all over me bubbled to the surface. Blood roared in my ears. Breath came short and choppy. I felt his weight across my chest, his pawing hands, smelled his sweat and polecat breath. But it weren't a feeling of helplessness or blind fear that washed over me this time. No, this time it was steaming-hot rage.

The jaguar sleeping deep inside me stirred, pinned her ears flat and switched her tail. An itching feeling inside my belly made me shudder. Thunder roared, clouds split in half, and rain poured. I knew right off my anger was fixing to whup up a fury the likes of which the delta had never seen. I ran out from under the porch roof and stood in the downpour to cool the fire raging inside me.

"Bethany Ann. Come in out of the rain." Benjamin's voice of reason smothered the flames.

Soaking wet, I walked past him into the cabin. He didn't follow, just waited for me to put on dry clothes and come back outside. We sat quiet. I figured Benjamin understood my rage had conjured the storm and the panther inside had almost clawed her way out. He was either trying to come to terms with it, was lost for words, or scared stupid. The rainstorm passed leaving everything smelling sweet and washed clean. He glanced over at me.

"Sometimes you scare the hell out of me, Bethany Ann."

"Yeah, figured so." I met his gaze. "Still want me to take them dark pieces out of the box?"

"No." His voice trembled. "But I haven't got a choice."

"So be it then. Tell me more about this favor you be needin'."

"Remember when you told me your mama never got sick and just died out of the blue?"

I studied him close. "Yeah."

"Well, that's just what happened to mine."

He shifted and took a deep breath.

"I think Lucius…Jedidiah murdered her so he could have Danni all to himself, and I think he did the same to your mama so he could have you."

He might as well thrown a bucket of ice water in my face. He waited for me to say something, but I couldn't do nothing but stare.

"I can't prove it, but you can."

"How?"

An uneasy look washed over his face, and he stuttered. "I…I…I have something I need to tell you. Before I came here the first time, I talked to a fortune teller in town."

"Lady Tibatha."

Looking grumpy and put out he grumbled, "I should've figured y'all know one another."

Rather put out myself, I snapped back. "What's that supposed to mean? Everybody in these here parts knows Lady Tibatha, and how she helped the Sheriff find that escaped jailbird years back."

"Sorry. I just thought…"

"You just thought that because she can see the future, and I can see haints that we're in cahoots together. Except for seeing her conjure that Voodoo god out of a lightning bolt, I ain't never talked to that voodoo woman.

"Are you telling me she was the Voodoo priestess in the white dress that night?"

I busted out laughing at the surprised look on his face. "For a lawman, you ain't too savvy on somethings, are ya."

"That isn't fair, Bethany Ann. I wasn't my usual self that night. I'm sorry I thought all of you…mystical folks were members of some huge supernatural community. Can we get on with this?"

It were easy to forgive him. "Go on."

"Like I was saying, Lady Tibatha told me some things about you."

"What kinda things?"

"She said you were a daughter of the Howling Moon, that you're half spirit and you can walk through dimensions."

"What does dimensions mean?"

"Different worlds. At the time I didn't believe one word of it. But since then, I've seen stuff that's changed my mind."

He ran his hand through his hair. "I can't believe I'm saying this." He took a deep breath. "I need you to go wherever it is that dead people go, find Mom, and ask her how she died."

If he'd kissed me full on the mouth, I couldn't have been more shocked. I shook my head. His hand shot out and grabbed my wrist.

"Bethany Ann, you must."

The sheer worry in his voice was another surprise. Why was this so important to him? Curious, I asked, "Why?"

"Don't you want to know if he killed your mother?"

I didn't for one minute think that was the true reason, but he was in such a tizzy, I didn't press him. "Jedidiah Wayne ripped the heart and soul out of Mama years ago. She'd been walking around dead for a long time."

Benjamin's eyes could say more than all his words put together. Dreamboat eyes was what Sarah Rose would've call them. Big and blue, hidden under long, dark lashes. Sometimes cold, others times skittish, but more often, gentle. I could read them easy as falling off a log backwards. What they were saying now damn-near broke my heart. I covered his hand with mine, and my words lost their sting.

"Knowing if he killed her won't change nothing, Benjamin. It won't bring her back to ya."

His hand dropped, and so did his voice. "Don't you

think I know that? It's just that even after all this time, Danni still won't let me go. I could never understand why, until now. She led me here so I could uncover the truth. But I can't do it alone. Please, Bethany Ann."

If you asked me how Soul-Latching works, I'd be hard-pressed to tell ya. My eyes didn't close, but I lost all sight. Swamp noises of birds singing, mosquitoes buzzing, gators floppin' and flippin' fell silent. I turned myself inside out and trusted only feelings to guide me. In that shadow land between sky and earth, our souls reached out and latched on to one another. I saw grayness around his heart. Felt his sorrow, his anguish, but most of all the guilt that tossed and turned in him every waking minute and tore a hole in his gut. Benjamin's soul cried out for help. I'd be lower than an egg-suckin' dog if I didn't at least try to find a way to ease his torment.

His face came back to me.

"Bethany Ann? Will you do it? For me?"

"I'll do my best, Benjamin, but to be honest, I ain't never done nothing like this before. Haints usually seek me out, not the other way around."

It was then that the sun came out behind the clouds and the golden rays hit the heart locket I wore around my neck. I smiled. Mama always found a way to tell me what to do. "Do you have anything of your mama's?"

"Like what?"

"Anything. A ring or necklace."

"I have this." He reached into his back pocket and pulled out a leather wallet. His strong hands trembled when he opened the billfold and handed me a folded-up piece of yellowed paper.

"It's the only picture I have of her. Be careful with it. It's old and worn out. I used to look at it every day until it got a big fold line down the middle. Now I'm scared to. Afraid it will tear in half."

I smoothed out the tiny lines and creases around a smiling face. My fingers skipped over her likeness. "She has a kind soul. A healing soul."

"Mom was a nurse."

"She took care of the ones others shunned."

"Yeah. She worked with the tuberculosis patients."

I glanced up at him. "Tuberculosis?"

He fumbled for a minute. 'Consumption."

I nodded in understanding. "You have her eyes."

Impatient, or more likely embarrassed, he tugged at his collar. "What do you need me to do?"

I pointed at the corner. "I need you to sit over there and lean your back against the railing. Shut your eyes and bring her out of memory. See her face. Smell her soap. Feel her arms wrapped round you. Remember how loved and safe that made you feel. Don't let any bad in. Hold on only to the good. If you can do that, I'll do the rest."

He started over to the side of the porch then stopped dead in his tracks.

Darkness.

Looked like the dead of night in the middle of the day. Something had done gone and stole all the light. Sarah Rose and me had seen the same thing happen when we was nine years old. Won't never forget it. Folks called it an eclipse. But knowing what was going on didn't stop my skin from turning into gooseflesh.

"And Moses stretched forth his hand toward heaven, and there was a thick darkness in all the land."

Benjamin growled, "Christ's sake, Bethany Ann, don't start quoting scripture on me."

I giggled, but not because I was tickled. Being plunged into dark right before I was going to step over into the world of the dead made my nerves jump like a frog on a hot rock. "It ain't nothing hurtful, just an eclipse."

He threw me a look as if wondering who I was trying to convince. His growl turned into a bite. "I know what the hell it is. But don't ya think it's a little strange it's happening now? "

About that time, a long, soulful howl came from deep in the wilds. The goose bumps on my arm turned to little icy hairs sticking straight up. Not because I was scared. But because I was excited. A wolf in the swamp. Couldn't wait to see him.

Benjamin's hand reached for the pistol on his hip. It hit home then that even though it was his idea that I cross over into a different world, he was spooked good. If this was gonna work, we'd both have to calm down.

"Benjamin, that ain't no hobgoblin. It's only a wolf, that's all. He's mixed up 'cause it turned night during the heat of the day."

He eased down and leaned his back against the cabin's door. I heard him mumble, "Shit fire. First a jaguar, now a wolf. What next? A pink elephant?"

Even if it were a little mean, I couldn't help but tease him. "Why you sitting in the middle of the porch with your back against the door instead by the railing?"

"Training. First thing a lawman learns is always face front."

"So you can see what the boogeyman looks like right before he gobbles ya up?"

He laughed then and the color came back to his face. I felt the tightness in his shoulders ease. Eyes closed, he sighed, "Ok. I'm ready."

I couldn't help one last jab. "Benjamin? I need you to do one more thing for me, and it's real important."

"Anything. What is it?"

"Breathe."

Surrounded in charcoal shadows and goose-flesh silence, I pressed the picture between my palms and closed my eyes.

Chapter 22

One miserably hot August night, a traveling preacher man from up Mobile way came through town and joined up with one of Jedidiah's revivals. Reverend Bob's claim to fame was that he had drowned and gone to heaven only to be turned away at the Pearly Gates. He said God sent him back to testify to the masses that there was indeed everlasting life and to sing the praises of the glory of heaven.

According to Reverend Bob, the roads in heaven were not made of gold but of glass, so that the dearly departed could look down upon their loved ones any time they pleased. He also testified that there were many rooms in heaven. One room was full of legs. Another had arms. Others were full of hands and feet. This was so if you had lost a piece of your body, when you got to heaven, you could get it back and be whole again. That notion tickled the fire out of me. I'd seen my share of angels. They were made of golden light and pure love. Weren't no need of them having arms or legs or anything human.

I ain't got no idea what part of heaven Reverend Bob had been in. The part I stepped over into was completely different. I reckon'd heaven was in the eye of the beholder. Maybe to a sea captain, heaven would be a huge ocean with crystal blue water stretching as far as the eye could see, and he could sail forever with fair winds and calm water. A farmer's idea of heaven might be rows and rows of ripe yella corn growing in rich, dark soil with endless days of beautiful sunshine and no drought. I hadn't really given much thought about what heaven would look like, which was good 'cause what I saw before me was more beautiful than anything I could've made up.

Acres and acres of waist-high green grass rippled in a soft breeze that smelled like fresh-cut hay right after a spring rain. A pale blue sky was full of fat, white-dumpling clouds. Colors popped so bright, I swear they was alive. I could taste the fresh, crisp green, shiver in the icy blue and bask in the warm yellow. I couldn't help but think this was how the very first colors looked when God named them. Sharp. Clean. Brilliant. The dingy film of the lower world had been peeled away from my eyes, and I saw the untainted, unspoiled, pure beauty and love that was God.

Maybe she had been there all along, and until that hazy film had been stripped away, I hadn't been able to see her. But there she stood only a few steps from me. Dressed in a pink gown, she looked like a beautiful rose caught in heaven's brilliant glow. I knew right off it was Benjamin's mama.

"Hello, Bethany Ann." Her voice a soft purr. "Let's sit."

And just like that, two oversized high-back wicker chairs with soft cushions came into sight. Sarah Rose and me had seen those chairs once in a Montgomery Ward catalog. We pretended we was rich, uppity society folk drinking our cool drinks sitting in them white chairs. Now here I was sitting in one underneath a tree so big I'd have to name it great-great-great grandpa cypress.

Butterflies flitted round my head, and birds perched on the back of the chair. Rabbits and deer chewed on that high grass only an arm's reach from me, unafraid and tame.

Reverend Bob's heaven didn't have no animals on account of pigs. The story goes thatJesus cast some demons into a bunch of swine and they had run down a steep hill and drowned in the sea. So naturally everybody jumped to the conclusion that pigs were evil, and because of that, no critters could go to heaven, which was another notion that was plumb stupid. Jesus's most favorite things was little children and animals because of their innocence and love.

I was mighty glad that, at least in my heaven, there was plenty of critters running around.

I gazed over at her. "Do you know why I'm here?"

"Benjamin."

"Yes, ma'am."

Now that the time had come to ask her how she died, I balked. Didn't seem right to ask such an awful question and spoil the goodness of this holy place, but Benjamin was counting on me. Even so, I ducked my head and mumbled his suspicion.

"He thinks you got murdered."

Her smile didn't exactly run away, but it didn't stay put neither. "We don't dwell on such things here. It isn't important."

"Yes, ma'am, I understand, but in the lower world it's real important, especially to him. He has to know for his own peace of mind."

She frowned then and clicked her tongue. "Until Benjamin understands that a person chooses their own destiny, he will never have peace of mind. No matter how good the intent, no one can change another's life. He blames himself for Danni's crossing, but it was her choice to make, not his.

"His soul is so heavy with the burden of guilt and blame over Danni's so-called death and mine, that in order to lighten the load, he threw God and faith out of his heart. Now, he's not only lost peace of mind but his way as well."

She shook her head, and for the first time since coming here, I felt sad.

"My answer to his question will not give him the peace he seeks."

That pretty well told me all I needed to know. "Guess that means you were kilt."

I bit my lip.

Good bet Mama was too.

Finding out that Jedidiah killed Mama should've thrown me into a wall-eyed hissy fit,but it didn't. I only felt calmness surround me. No rage. No hate. Guess she was right. In heaven, those things just didn't matter. Of course, when I got back to the lower world, all that would change real quick.

Something wet hit my arm. All around me there came a soft whispering. I ran out from in under the tree and watched hundreds of glass ornaments float down from the sky. I heard her laugh behind me.

"What are they?" I asked.

"Raindrops."

Good God Almighty, the rainbow must have shattered into pieces. Each drop was the color of orange, green, blue, and red. And different shapes too. Circles, crescent-moons, and diamonds. Every time one landed on my skin, it would pop like a soap-bubble and pure joy and rapture spread over my body. The scent of sharp peppermint, and fresh strawberries swirled all around. Felt like I was sitting smack-dab in the middle of one of those fancy heart- shaped boxes of chocolates that Baker Emporium sold at Valentines.

I had to dance and play in those crystal raindrops or split apart at the seams. I ran. Twirled. Laughed until my sides ached.

Reverend Bob had one thing right, only the power of God could make a body leave this place.

I grinned at her. "I love it here."

"You are a daughter of the Howling Moon, Bethany Ann. You can return here anytime you wish just by closing your eyes and thinking it so, but for now, you must go. You've been here too long, and Benjamin is tired."

"What? I only just got here."

"Time stops in this place, but I speak true. You've been away half a day and must return to Benjamin. He needs you. You are his salvation."

His salvation? How was I supposed to save him? Pretty tall order if'n you asked me.

It was then I felt his tug. The dull film of the lower world started to cover my eyes once more and block out all sight of her. Before she completely disappeared, I yelled out.

"He could use a sign, ya know."

Her form faded.

"Don't have to be a big one," I shouted. "When you're lost, even a little sign means a lot."

I didn't have to open my eyes to know I was back. Benjamin's hand lay heavy on my arm, and I couldn't feel my butt.

Chapter 23

Split-in-halves are souls that make a pact of strong friendship long before they step into human skin. Sometimes they stay tied together and are called twins. Most the time, however, they split and go in different directions. No matter how long they might wander alone, split-in-halves are never lost from their other half. That's why a stranger can look so familiar. Why close friendships be made within seconds. Their bond is golden, blessed by all that is holy. It's a special tie that can't be unraveled and no power on heaven or earth can destroy. It's rare split-in-halves remember their other while in human form. They feel a kinship to the other and a strong bond, but can't put their finger on why.

Benjamin was my split-in-half.

Course, he had no idea of this notion and I weren't going to explain it. But. I knew.

I felt his warm breath on my skin, smelled his scent of wood and rain. It weren't no surprise when I finally gave in and opened my eyes. His face was only a whisper away from mine. The look of hope in those dreamboat eyes sent a knife through my heart. How could I soften the truth? Shield him from pain? How could I tell him that his suspicions had been right? That his mama's life had been cut short by the very man she trusted as a husband and who he'd called daddy?

"Benjamin…"

"You don't have to say anything, Bethany Ann. The tears on your cheeks tell me all I need to know."

Surprised, I touched the side of my face. I didn't know I'd been crying. He moved away. I stood. Tiny needles of feeling came back into my rear end. How long had I been sittin'? Must've been a good while. The creepy darkness of the eclipse had given way to bright sunlight once more. He turned back to me.

"You really saw her?"

"I really did." I answered his next question before he asked it. "She's at peace, Benjamin. She's a little worried about you though."

"Nothing new about that." He tilted his head. "Did you see your mother as well?"

"I don't have to go to another realm to see Mama," I said and rubbed the blood back into my legs. "She's with me all the time."

"You really believe that, don't you?"

"I know it."

His sigh came low and drawn out. "Oh, Bethany Ann, I wish I had just a pinch of your faith and goodness."

Goodness? I choked down a wicked laugh. Oh, if he only knew. Knew how strong my heart beat with cold revenge. The peace that had surrounded me in heaven was a world away. Forgiveness had dissolved into nothing. Jedidiah killed Mama. Anger boiled and bubbled in the pit of my belly. Righteous anger Mama would've called it. Whether it be righteous or not didn't mean spit to me.

I would kill Jedidiah Wayne.

An eye for an eye—ain't that what the Good Book said?

I handed his mama's picture back to him. "I'm sorry, Benjamin."

He took the photo and shook his head. "I'm sorry for you, too."

I turned to go back into the cabin.

"What did you do?"

His fierce tone made me jump.

"What?"

"To the picture. What did you do?"

My heart leaped straight into my gullet. Lord, God, had I held the photo too tight between my palms? Had it ripped it in half? I'd never forgive myself for ruining the only thing he had left of his mama. "What are ya talkin' about?"

"Look at it. It's brand new."

I took the picture and gasped. No big fold line down the middle. The smile of the woman before me leaped off the paper as if the picture had been taken only hours ago.

Hours ago.

I had to hand it to Benjamin's mama. It was one hell of a sign.

"How did you do that?" he asked.

"I didn't, Benjamin." I handed the picture back. "She did."

He just stared. I could see him trying to make sense of it all. Not quite believing, but wanting to something fierce. I felt his tears. I knew he rather take a beating then cry in front of me, so I slipped into the cabin and made a big show of putting the canned goods on the shelf. Every once in a while, I'd peek out the screen door. He sat on the porch steps, his back turned to me, but I saw his broad shoulders rise and fall. I waited a few minutes more then went out and eased down beside him.

Early dusk crept slowly into the wetlands. One-by-one as if by magic, evening stars broke through the fading light and twinkled and blinked in the gentle breeze. The scent of magnolia and honeysuckle hung so heavy, I could taste it on the tip of my tongue.

It was the time of day when all things unexplained came out of shadow to kneel before the altar of the Church of the Howling Moon.

The sharp glare of the real world yielded to the mist and mystery of twilight. The onion-skin veil between them dimensions Benjamin had talked about weakened and souls stepped over the line with ease. The heat of the sun surrendered to coolness of the moon. Reason gave way to instinct and knowing. The blood in my veins ran hot, and I itched to dance in the moonlight and run side-by-side with the wind.

I shut my eyes and caught Benjamin's soul.

For the first time ever, I felt a dash of hope in his heart.

He reached over, took my hand in his, and gave my fingers a small squeeze. We sat quiet for a spell listening to the sound of the night and holding hands. But not in a courting kind of way. Split-in-halves never marry or have romantic feelings between them. Benjamin would always be extra-special to me and we were willing to die for the other. But he would never be my beau, or me, his.

"Nice night, ain't it?" I whispered.

He said nothing. Didn't have to.

The tears on his cheek told me everything I needed to know.

Chapter 24

Night black as pitch. Deafening silence fell all around Ben.

Eyes, wide and white in mud-smeared faces.

The gritty, bitter taste of gunpowder flavored dry lips. Choked. Smothered.

The stink of sweat.

Nerves danced. Hands and wrists ached from clutching rifles close.

They waited. Hunkered down in the fighting hole.

They waited. For the scream of shells to rip the night apart.

Waited for the zip of bullets to whiz past.

Waited. For Death to jump into the hole and tap their shoulders.

Waiting for battle in a foxhole made grown men cry. All prayed. Even the non-believers. After surviving that horror show, Ben thought nothing could scare him ever again, but that damn eclipse had fried his nerves to a crisp. Just a strange twist of fate. Right? Lady Tibatha's voice came back to him, "There'd be no coincidences."

Not for one minute did he truly believe Bethany Ann could travel to another dimension and find the dead. Yet he'd asked her anyway. Why? Desperate men do desperate things.

He'd sat alone for half a day surrounded in inky blackness with wolf howls and hair-raising screech owls keeping him company and waited for Bethany Ann to snap out of whatever trance she was in. Tears leaked from the corners of her eyes and trickled down her face. He actually felt her heart ache for him. That never happened before. Skeptical and doubting, he turned away. Then she handed him the picture.

Mom's picture robbed him of sleep.

He bought a silver frame with pink roses around the edge to preserve the photo under pressed glass. Something told him however, he'd be aged and cracked long before the picture would show any signs of wear.

The photo was a cold, hard slap of reality upside his face, and it rattled him to the bone. She told him it was sign from Mom. Still he doubted. But how could he deny the proof he held in his hands? A dam of emotions broke loose inside him and spewed forth. For the first time in years, he dared to believe in a power greater than himself. Maybe not whole-hog. Not yet. But enough to where he was able to sit in peace beside a girl mysterious as twilight.

He walked to work. Not because it was a pretty day. Just the opposite. It was another hot, humid, sticky morning. His starched uniform shirt wilted five minutes after he walked out the door. But because he needed time. Time to process and make sense out of everything that had happened.

Lost in thought, he barely missed being trampled by the tall middle-aged man who came stomping out of the sheriff's office. Something familiar about the guy, but he couldn't place him. He pushed open the door and walked into the office.

"Boss? Who was that?"

Something was wrong. Buford's usual smile

flattened into a thin line. "That there was John Wesley."

Benjamin repeated the name in his head. He'd heard it before. But where?

Buford pushed back his chair, stood, and raked thin hair with stubby fingers. "This is serious, Ben. Wesley's niece, Hanna been missing for two days."

It hit him then. "Boss, that girl at the river was named Hanna. I thought she was Wesley's daughter."

"She might as well be. Hanna is John's sister's young'un. Ruby Miller is as wild as a March hare. All she can do to take care of herself. A kid just got in her way. John and his wife allowed as how they could take better care of the child, so they went up to Shreveport last summer and fetched the girl. Now she's gone missing." He glanced over at Ben. "I got a bad feeling on this one."

The air left the room.

"Ben?"

The sheriff's voice sounded a mile away. The room spun. Knees buckled. He slumped into the straight-back chair and struggled for a deep breath. What had Bethany Ann said? Hanna Miller would be the first Jedidiah would come for?

Buford pounded his back.

"Ben? You having a heart attack on me, son?"

How? How could've he forgotten Bethany Ann's warning? Wasn't his fault. He thought the girl's name was Hanna Wesley. Honest mistake. Wasn't it?

"Ben? Ben!"

Buford shook him like a rag doll. Christ if he *had* been in a middle of a heart attack, the boss's shaking and pounding would've thrown him in the grave. He pushed the sheriff aside and leapt to his feet.

"He's got her, Buford. That son-of-a-bitch's got her."

"Who?'

"Jedidiah Wayne."

Ben raced behind the desk and tore open the middle drawer. Frantic, he rummaged through the packages of Juicy Fruit, toothpicks, and loose paperclips. "Where the hell are they?"

"What?"

"The keys to the gun cabinet. I'm not going after Wayne with only a revolver."

"Damn it, Ben. Stop!

He'd never heard the boss yell before. Brought-up short, he quit digging in the drawer and lifted his gaze.

"Ben, this vendetta you got against Wayne is getting out-of-hand. I only got your word to go on that he's rotten to the core. We ain't got no proof he's harmed anyone."

He slammed the drawer shut so hard the wooden desk shook on its legs. "Buford, you don't understand. Bethany Ann told me he'd come after Hanna Miller. I never made the connection. Thought the girl's name was Wesley."

"And just how does Bethany Ann know this?"

"She had a vision"

Even to his own mind the words sounded ridiculous. No wonder Buford stood gawking at him.

"Boy, do you know how loony that sounds?"

"I imagine it sounds just as crazy as it did that day Lady Tibatha told you what she'd seen. But it didn't stop you from going after that convict. Why? Why did you believe her when no one else did?"

From the hang-dog expression on the sheriff's face,

he knew the question had hit the mark. The big man's voice softened. "Can't explain why. I just did."

"How's this any different?"

The big lawman fumbled in his pants pocket. He tossed a set of keys to Ben. "Grab an extra box of shells, too."

Buford poured the coals to the Ford. Even still, Ben resisted the urge to reach over with his boot and tromp down on the accelerator. Sweat trickled down the side of his face. He wiped it away with his bare arm. The steeple of Wayne's church came into view. The sheriff slowed and gazed over at him.

"Get a hold of yourself, Ben. We ain't got no proof, and you know how revered Jedidiah Wayne is to his followers. We don't want to rush in half-cocked and get ourselves in a mess we can't get out of."

He nodded, but Buford might as well have been pissing into the wind. Before the White Rose rolled to a stop, Ben flung open the heavy door and bolted toward the church. Jedidiah Wayne met him half way. Ben grabbed him up by the shirt front.

"Where is she, you bastard?"

Wayne's dumbass expression hit like kerosene on flame. A sharp right cross to the jaw sent lightning shooting up Ben's arm, but the satisfaction of seeing the preacher sprawled in the dirt made the pain worthwhile.

Get up you bastard. I dare ya. Get up and turn the other cheek. I'll break that side of your face too.

Blood oozed from the corner of Wayne's mouth. He struggled to his knees.

Ben stood tall over him.

"Don't play stupid with me, Jedidiah. Or should I say Lucius?"

A flicker. Only a flicker of an eye betrayed Wayne's recognition of him. A glimmer invisible to everyone. Except Ben.

He hauled the preacher to his feet. His hand curled into a fist ready to slam Wayne's jaw again, but his arm wouldn't move. Buford held him with an iron grip. Who would've thought underneath all that bulk lurked such strength?

"Let him go, son."

The sheriff's voice came low and calm, but he heard the cold warning in the words. The last thing he wanted was to make an enemy out of Sheriff Buford Tate. He took a step back.

"Jedidiah," Buford said. "You'll have to excuse my deputy. We're hunting for a missing girl. It's hotter than billy-blue-blazes out here and emotions are running full bore. I'm sure you understand."

Ben bit his lip.

Wayne wiped the blood off his chin and straightened his shirt. "Father, forgive them; for they know not what they do. Luke 23:34."

A vein in the sheriff's thick neck throbbed.

Ben fumed. How dare this sick, twisted hypocritical piece of shit equate himself to the Son of God? Wasn't that a sin? Blasphemy? He lunged at Wayne.

Buford's hand smacked his chest.

Must have been a funny sight. A whip thin preacher, a tall, muscular deputy and a fat roly-poly sheriff standing in the middle. The metallic clicking sound behind him made the hairs on the back of his neck stand up. Slow and cautious, he turned.

Hester Wayne stood not more than three feet away holding a shotgun with barrels bigger than telephone poles.

A shotgun aimed at his head with the hammers pulled back.

"Sheriff Tate." Her voice oozed venom. "We shoot rabid animals around these-here parts. Best you throw a rope on that dog of yours and haul him out of here."

Buford dropped his arm and nudged Ben toward the car.

That was it? He couldn't believe the boss wasn't going to say anything. Well, he sure as hell wouldn't slink away, tail tucked between his legs. He whirled on Wayne.

"This isn't the end of it, Lucius. You might have all these folks around here fooled, but I know who you are and what you've done. I swear, if it's the last thing I do, I'll see you fry."

He beat the sheriff back to the cruiser and slid behind the wheel instead the passenger's seat. Buford barely had time to swing his legs in before Ben gunned the Ford and tore down the road leaving a rooster tail of thick dust behind them.

The air in the car snapped and crackled. Why? Why hadn't the boss backed him up? They hadn't gone a mile before Buford rummaged in the glove box and pulled out a flask. He unscrewed the top. The scent of pure-grain alcohol bit the air. The sheriff took a long pull. Shocked, Ben pulled the car underneath a shade tree and eased into neutral.

"Moonshine's illegal."

"Arrest me."

His laugh broke the tension.

Buford took another hit and smacked his lips. "Ben, I swear to God you could piss off the Pope. Weren't no cause to light into Wayne like you did especially after me telling ya to go slow. You're the best young deputy I've ever seen, and I truly admire that burning desire you have to see justice done." He wiped his mouth on the back of his hand. "Yes sir. I truly do respect that about you. But you need to put a tight rein on that temper of yours 'cause in this neck of the woods it's liable to get you killed. You're lucky that stringy piece of crow bait, Hester Wayne didn't blow your head plumb off and mine too just for good measure."

"You really think she would've shot me? A deputy sheriff?"

"Get this through your head, boy. Hester Wayne worships the ground her brother walks on and hates the dirt you stand in. She itched to pull the trigger."

He offered the flask to Ben. "Son, I may be just an old backwoods parish sheriff, but I have managed to learn a thing or two in my twenty years of wearing a badge. I saw that slice of fear cut across Wayne's eyes. Not once did he ask who the girl was or deny anything. 'Course your fist upside his head had a lot to do with that. But Wayne is an arrogant SOB who likes to play God. He thinks he's above the law. His pride and overconfidence could've made him careless. Made him say something that would of incriminated himself or let something slip about Hanna's whereabouts. Now, we'll never know."

If Buford wanted to him to feel lower than dirt, then the sheriff had succeeded. "Sorry boss. Guess I still have a thing or two to learn."

Ben took a sip of the white dog. The clear liquid burned his throat raw and helped wash down the crow he just ate. He gave the container to the sheriff. The small pint went back into the glove compartment. Ben glanced over at the big man. "Do you think Wayne kidnapped Hanna?"

"Too early to say."

"Well, let me ask you this, then. What's your backwoods parish sheriff's gut telling ya?"

"He's guilty as sin."

"Your gut ever wrong?"

"Not often."

Ben shifted into drive. "We won't find her alive, ya know."

Buford let out a long sigh. "Yep. I know."

The ride back to town was a long one. And silent.

Chapter 25

The idea of changing into a bird hit me one afternoon when I was guttin' catfish. Crows always waited in the trees for the innards I threw to them. One grew bold and flew down close to watch. I named him Ichabod, on account of Sarah Rose.

One Halloween, Miss Hanagan read us a story *The Legend of Sleepy Hollar*, and Sarah Rose fell in love with Ichabod Crane. She said when she grew up and got hitched she was goin' to name her first boy child Ichabod. Because I'd been thinking a lot about Sarah Rose and because I just liked saying the name, that's what I called the crow.

I studied the way Ichabod swooped down from the trees with wings spread like black sails. Quiet as night. He'd strut his stuff, steal a piece of fish, then lift off into the air smooth as silk. That set me to thinkin' on the notion of flying.

Course I didn't have any idea on how to turn into a bird. The jaguar had just happened. When angry or cornered, I'd feel a fierce itch start deep in my belly, and before I knowed it, I was a jungle cat. Becomin' some other kind of animal or bird on purpose was something else entirely.

One muggy morning, Ichabod lit on the porch rail, cocked his head at me, and set to cawing. Got the feeling he was telling me to get off that porch and fly. I fixed my mind on him. Just him. Nothing else. Trees blurred. Sounds stopped. Everything started to spin. Felt dizzy, fuzzy headed and it happened.

Good God Almighty. Ever ride a Radio Flyer Wagon downhill so fast it takes the breath plumb out of ya? Your innards disappear. You're scared and silly-minded all at the same time, and can't wait to do it all over again? Flying was just like that, only a heap better. With only a small flap of my wings, I could sail on the wind's back and cover half the bayou in nothing flat.

First place I headed for was Jedidiah's.

Nobody knew how many times I'd perched on the limbs of this tree. Nobody. Not Mama. Not even Sarah Rose. The sweet smelling magnolia stood tall and out-of-place next to the old stinking barn. I'd climb its branches when it were too hot to stay inside or too dark to run to the swamp. Hidden by thick, shiny leaves, Jedidiah's harsh words and slaps couldn't find me. Too bad Mama didn't climb trees. If'n she had…well that didn't matter now. Kinda' funny she was resting for all eternity underneath the very tree that had protected me, and I'd shared so many secrets with.

Not even a rough wooden cross marked the grave. Weren't right. Granny Polly, PaPa Joe, and Mama's oldest brother, Roy Robert, were laid side-by-side in the family vault at the cemetery down the road a piece. Mama should've been with them. Their tomb weren't nothing fancy, but it sure beat a wet mound of earth that didn't even tell who was under the dirt.

Bet Aunt Hester was to blame for Mama not being with kin. She hated Mama. Never could figure out why. Once Mama said it was because Hester felt threatened by her. I had no idea what that meant.

Usually I didn't pay no heed to Aunt Hester. Folks can't choose their kin. But the day she tried to drown Sissy Cat's babies changed all that.

I'd seen what she was fixin to do in a vision. Seen her sneakin out to the barn, tow sack in her hand, and killin' on her mind. So the next morning I was ready for her. Me and Sarah Rose hid under the bridge and waited. Soon as that gunny sack hit the water, me and her jumped in and saved every one of those little darlings.

I ran lickity-split back to the barn. Grabbed up Sissy and high-tailed it to Granny LaBeaux's barn. Maybe ol' Granny did have dried up heads hanging in every window, but it was a well-known fact she loved all animals and wouldn't hurt a hair on their heads.

I was late doing chores, and when I got home Aunt Hester read me the riot act. Didn't pay no mind to what she jabbered. I was too busy trying to figure out what that sticky, gooey black stuff was that surrounded her heart.

Evilness. Plain as day. I saw evil.

First time I'd ever seen vile wickedness in a body. Scared the liver plumb out of me. When she reached out and grabbed my arm pulling me into the kitchen, I reared back. Before I knew it the words, "Zezebel" flew out of my mouth. Whoo-ee. Jedidiah bout stripped off all my hide over that one. But it were worth it.

From that day on, Aunt Hester and me were enemies. I'd seen her true colors. Knew the goodness she smeared on thick as honey at meeting was just an act. That deep inside she had a mean streak a country mile long and the devil ruled her heart.

And she knew I knew.

Guess thinking about Hester conjured her up because about that time she walked out the back door with a basket of clothes to hang on the line. I wanted to swoop down and peck her bony head so bad I could taste it. Instead I let out a loud squawk. I liked being a crow. I couldn't visit Mama's grave in broad daylight as a panther but no one gave a second glance at a black crow sitting on a wood fence.

I watched her pin bed clothes to the line. Grandma's very quilt that I'd curled into all warm and snuggly. Didn't seem right, her touching the soft cloth. The screen door slammed shut. Jedidiah strolled out into the sunshine. His usual slick-back hair fell uncombed around his thin face and he hitched up his trousers which seemed awful peculiar to me. Looked like he just rolled out of bed. But in the middle of the day?

Aunt Hester acted funny too. She ducked her head in a shy sorta' way and smiled. Never, ever seen her do that before. Shoot, I'd bet good money her face would split apart at the seams if'n she grinned. Then she did something that made every bone in my tiny bird body turn to brittle sticks.

She sidled up to Jedidiah, leaned into his body, and kissed him full on the mouth.

Chapter 26

It had only been a few hours after flying home and turning back into my old self again when Benjamin showed up. Had a notion he'd turn up soon, but I didn't figure on him bringing Sheriff Buford Tate with him. Red-faced, huffing and puffing, the sheriff plopped his beefy butt down on the porch steps and leaned into the rail.

"Whoo-wee, hot out, ain't it?" He wiped the sweat from his round face with a handkerchief as big as a baby diaper.

"Let me fetch ya some cool water." I glanced at Benjamin who hadn't said two words since he introduced the sheriff to me. Weren't like him to be so quiet. Figured the dragon had wrung the starch plumb out of him. The worry lines around his eyes and the way he clenched that square jaw of his made me wonder if something bad was going on. My stomach started to churn. Course, that weren't nothing new. My belly had pitched and rolled ever since I'd seen Aunt Hester kiss her own brother.

I walked out back where I kept the water bucket. Out of eyesight, I stood silent and closed my eyes. In my head I pictured trees swaying back and forth in a gentle wind. Smelled the fresh scent of oncoming rain. Then I took a deep breath and blew it out while I twirled in a circle.

By the time I walked back to the front of the cabin, the clouds hid the sun and a cool breeze had kicked up. I smiled to myself. I was just learnin' how to change the sun and wind. Most of the time, I couldn't do it. Tickled the fire out of me when I did. I handed the cup to the sheriff who slurped up the water in deep gulps. He wiped his mouth with the back of his hand and grinned.

"Miss Bethany, that sure did hit the spot. Thank ya, kindly."

I'd never been called Miss anything ever. Not sure I liked it.

"Bethany Ann, I need you to tell the sheriff about your dream." Benjamin cleared his throat. "The dream about the murdered girls."

I stared deep into Benjamin's eyes. So deep I about lost myself in their dark blue color. "Another girl be missin', ain't there."

Before he could answer, Sheriff Tate interrupted. "You familiar with the Wilkes clan live down Fanes Creek way?"

My gaze never left Ben's face. "Yes, sir. Went to school with two of 'em, Alice Ann and Rebecca Sue." I turned to the sheriff. "Rebecca Sue has strawberry blonde hair and eyes greener than a gourd. She be the one missin." It weren't a question.

"Yep. She's the one."

My stomach somersaulted, and I sank to the ground. Head down, I struggled for a deep breath. I'd seen Becky Sue in that dream. Heard her voice crying out in the blackness. Benjamin sat crossed-legged beside me.

"We haven't found Hanna, and I'm not holding on to any hope of finding Rebecca either. Bethany Ann, where are they?"

He didn't understand. Folks without the gift of Sight never understood. Visions were like ground-hugging fog. Gray. Shadowed. They might come crystal clear, but before ya could latch on to em', they'd twist and turn. Disappear. I'd seen muddy water. Seen bent, crooked trees. Even smelled fish, mud, crawdads, and death.

And I had seen them. The girls. Broken dolls with shattered faces bobbing in the water. But I had no notion of where the place was.

"I don't know where they be, Benjamin."

"Miss Bethany, if Jedidiah Wayne is behind all of this, we can't touch him, can't stop him lessen' we get proof."

"If?"

I jumped to my feet and gawked at the fat, roly-poly sheriff. "I tell you true, Sheriff Buford Tate, Jedidiah took em'. Ruined em'. Then killed em'. But."

"But what?" Benjamin asked.

"He might have someone helping him."

For a big man, Sheriff Tate could move damn fast. He was off the porch and by my side in a blink of an eye. Benjamin grabbed my arm, twirled me around to look at him.

"What are you talking about?"

It took all I had to tell him about the disgusting kiss. How Hester acted more like a wife than a sister. It made me feel bad. Dirty somehow. Nobody said nothing for what seemed a lifetime. The sheriff broke the silence.

"Well if that don't beat all."

Benjamin caught his breath.

"What is it, son?"

All the brown tan on Benjamin's face had done slipped off. Made his eyes pop even bluer against the pasty white skin.

"Just remembered something Lady Tibatha told me.

She said danger would come to the children from one who claims to be what they aren't. At the time I thought she was talking about Wayne. Him pretending to be a God-fearing man of the cloth while all the time he's nothing but a monster. But maybe she was talking about Hester. Boss, maybe we got this whole thing figured wrong."

Buford stroked his chin and frowned. "Sure would explain some things."

I looked at Benjamin. "What things?"

"Having your sister loving and kissing on ya like a...a...lover could scramble the way ya think on things. It could shed some light on why Jedidiah does what he does."

I couldn't believe what I was hearing. "You making excuses for him now?"

"Don't you wonder why he is the way he is?"

What was Benjamin thinking? "Hell, no. I don't wonder. "He's a devil spirit, Benjamin. Plain and simple. Maybe Hester puts the ideas in his head, who knows? It don't matter. He's still ruining and killing little girls."

"And you don't want to understand why?"

I'd about had it with Benjamin talking nonsense. I could feel blood pounding in my ears. Clouds swirled and thunder rumbled. If he didn't straighten up and start making sense, all hell was gonna break loose.

"Why? Bethany Ann, why don't you want to understand?"

"Because understanding leads to forgiving. Forgiving leads to forgetting. I ain't about to forget. Don't want to forget what he did to Sarah Rose. Never forget what he tried to do to me. Forget him killing Mama. And I sure as hell don't want to forget all them young'uns he ruined and killed. And while you're standing here wasting time trying to figure, forgive, and forget, he's probably grabbed another young'un."

"Now, Miss Bethany. It's a Christian man's duty to forgive. Why the Good Book even says 'forgive those who trespass against us.'"

That did it.

Lightning forked the sky and hit a tree a stone's throw from where Sheriff Tate stood.

The cypress split in half with a fearsome roar. The smell of sulfur hit me square in the face. Smoke rolled out from the tree's scorched center. Tate looked like he was about to piss his pants. Benjamin jumped. Fighting mad, I whirled on both of them.

"Christian? Being a good Christian don't mean you let the devil stomp all over ya.

Archangel Michael is about as Christian as they come but that don't stop him from pulling out a flaming sword and cutting a demon's ass in half when need be. Besides, I never claimed to be a Christian, and I ain't no saint. What I am is a daughter of the Howling Moon, and I bow before no man."

"Bethany Ann, Sheriff Tate didn't mean—"

"Shut up, Benjamin."

I had never, ever said those words my entire life. Mama would've slapped me silly for talking so disrespectful. Benjamin had never spoke harsh, and I hated being so mean. A twinge of shame niggled at me, but it weren't enough to make me apologize. Benjamin just plain didn't know how sly the devil was.

The devil would charm, sweet-talk, and promise a heap of riches in order to throw good folks off their guard. Make folks pity him. Make him human. And in doing so, give him chance-after-chance to change. Wickedness counted on the forgiving nature of folks. While they was busy making excuses and trying to understand, evil was busy twisting and robbing souls. The devil had no intention of being good. How could I make Benjamin understand that by making excuses for Satan, he was playing right into his hands?

I willed him to see my reasoning, but he was having none of it. Not meeting my gaze, he asked, "Do you really think everyone who's done wrong is evil? That they don't deserve a second chance?"

"I ain't talking about all wrong doers, Benjamin. Deep down inside I believe most folks want to do the right thing and feel regret for their misdeeds. What I'm talking about is the great enemy of God. The demons who tempt, murder, and suck every drop of righteousness plumb out of a man's bones. Jedidiah Wayne sold his soul to the devil long ago and that's all what matters."

The smell of smoke wrinkled my nose. The snap and crackle of burning wood sounded behind me.

Benjamin's voice came low and strained. "Bethany Ann, you're fixing to catch the whole swamp on fire."

I spat into my hand, rubbed my palms together, and lifted them toward the sky.

Rain poured.

The fire went out.

Chapter 27

"Hell's buckets, Ben. Why didn't you tell me that gal was a walking, talking stick of dynamite?"

Ben slid into the driver's seat of the jeep and gunned the engine. The sudden downpour of rain turned the swamp into a steam pot. Sticky, humid, sultry air pressed down on his chest. A deep breath was out of the question. Buford's face glowed like an overripe tomato. The sheriff had wheezed and panted every step back. Ben hung his head. He shouldn't have set such a quick pace, but he wanted to get the hell away from Bethany Ann. He'd seen her pissed before but this was different. This was full-blown raging anger too strong for the voice of reason to smother.

"She isn't usually that forceful."

Buford snorted and shot him a quick glance. "Did she really make lightning hit that tree? And the rain? Did she make it rain just by spitting into her hand?"

Ben shook his head. "I've never seen her control the weather like that before, but, yes. She did."

"How?"

It was Ben's turn to snort. "How the hell do I know?"

"Reckon it has something to do with her being a daughter of the Howling Moon."

Ben downshifted. "Lady Tibatha explain all that to you, too?"

144

"She may have mentioned it in passing."

"Boss, if you don't mind me asking, just what is your relationship with that woman?"

Shit. He shouldn't have asked that. Wasn't any of his business. He cringed and waited for the sheriff to tell him to go to hell. Buford didn't blink an eye at the question.

"Ben, every lawman worth his salt has at least one good informant. Tibby is mine. I've solved a lot of cases with information she's passed on to me. In return, I make sure no one bothers her kind."

"Her kind? You mean the coloreds?"

Buford's forehead puckered. "I mean Voodoo." The big man shifted in his seat. "I don't pretend to know squat about their beliefs, but as long as I've been sheriff of St. Clair Parish, I ain't had a lick of trouble with them folks. That's the reason why I never believed that cock and bull story Jedidiah Wayne told about them stealing his daughter and turning a wildcat loose on his face."

"Have you asked Tibb…I mean Lady Tibatha about finding the girls?"

"Yep. First thing I did. But the cards won't tell her."

"Why?"

"She says Bethany Ann has to find them, so *Loa* won't show her anything to help. Has something to do with the girl's destiny."

"Guess that's good in a way. Means she'll find them eventually."

"Eventually."

"Boss, what do you think about this new development with Hester Wayne? Where do you think she fits in with all of this?"

Buford heaved a deep sigh and stared out the car

window. "I ain't righty sure. For as long as I can remember Hester and Jedidiah been together. Just assumed they was brother and sister. Nobody ever said different. Suppose she could be his wife, just never occurred to me before."

"What if she isn't? His wife, I mean."

"Jesus Lord, Ben. You want me to puke right here and now?"

The thought left a sour taste in the back on Ben's throat too. "Wouldn't there be birth certificates or a wedding license or something on file we could check?"

"That's big city talk, Ben. Round these-here parts the family Bible is the only record of such things, and it ain't likely Jedidiah be too receptive to showing us his." Buford scratched his chin. "Course they might be one person who could shed some light on all this."

"Who?"

"Ezekiel Wayne. Jedidiah's brother."

"Never heard of him."

"Ezekiel keeps to hisself. Ol' Zeke don't have a whole lot to do with Jedidiah and his kin. Gotta be a reason for that."

"What are we waiting on, let's go talk to him."

"Now hold on, boy. Jedidiah ain't the only one Zeke don't cotton to. He don't have much use for most folks and there ain't a snowball's chance in hell, he'd open up and talk to us about kinfolk even if he don't like 'em. Blood's thicker than water, ya' know."

"Then what's the plan?"

"Zeke has two weaknesses."

Ben cocked an eyebrow and glanced at the sheriff. "Which are?"

"White Dog and coon hunting."

"How's that help us? Neither one of us hunt raccoons."

"Nope. But my cousin Leroy does. Come to think of it, he's paired up with Zeke a few times. Kinda likes the fella. You can be sure white lightning will be flowing heavy at any hunt. Leroy owes me a favor. Had a run in with the law down Bitterroot way. Nothing too serious. More a misunderstanding than anything. I got him off with only an apology. Think there's a hunt coming up in a day or two. I'll have Leroy get Zeke all liquored up. Ask him about family. See what he says."

Ben nodded. "Guess it's better than no plan at all."

The jeep growled and rumbled on the dirt road. A dark shape zipped out of the weeds and crossed in front of Ben. He stomped on the brakes to keep from hitting the critter.

"Feral cat." Buford unwrapped a piece of Juicy Fruit. "They live in that barn over yonder."

Ben followed the sheriff's finger. A faded red barn stood next to a boarded up house. An overgrown field surrounded a large pond nearby the barn. "Who lives there?"

"Nobody now. Used to belong to an old spinster named Ruby LaBeaux. Been vacant for years."

"Why? Looks like it was a nice place at one time. I bet with some good elbow grease it could be again."

"Folks think it's cursed. Granny LaBeaux was a *Voodioenne*, a voodoo priestess. No one wants any part of her or what belonged to her. It's a shame, really. It's a nice house with electricity, running water, even an inside bathroom. Good land and barn going to seed because of superstition and people's fear. It'd make a nice home for someone.

Nicer than a beat up ol' shack deep in the swamps. Ben shook his head at the thought. He doubted Bethany Ann would step one foot away from her wetland sanctuary. The sheriff broke into his thoughts.

"Ben, we got us a huge problem, son. Two girls missing. We both know Wayne's got something to do with it. But until we find them, our hands are tied. For all we know, they just decided to up and run away. We have to find those girls, Ben. Dead or alive. If it's up to Bethany Ann then you're gonna have to find a way to make that happen. And quick. I don't want to look another father in the eye and tell him we got nothing. Understand?"

Ben nodded. "Yes sir. I'll think of something."

He was glad Buford didn't ask what.

He had no idea.

Chapter 28

Ever get so riled up your innards shake and your head pounds? I lay flat on the hard porch floor and willed my heart to slow down before it broke my chest. The rain done put out the fire that scorched the weathered cypress, but did nothing to smother the flames burning inside me. It ain't like I'd never been angry before. Lord knows, my temper and sharp tongue could cut to the quick. But this untamed rage was something new.

To be fair, Benjamin taking up for Jedidiah was something I made up in my head. Never once had he said outright that Jedidiah wasn't evil. I knew he hated that no good egg-suckin' preacher man down to his toes, same as me. Also knew he'd never forget what the son-of-a-bitch did to his mama. Benjamin was just the kind of man who needed to know the how and why of things. He couldn't help it. God make him that way. Whereas me? I was cut from different cloth.

Benjamin questioned. I knew outright.

And while I was being truthful with myself, I had to admit that this fury churnin' in my gut wasn't all that strange. Anger had been simmering deep inside me for a while now. Benjamin and the Sheriff had only brought it to a boil. I wasn't mad at Benjamin. I was good and pissed with myself. I couldn't see where Hanna and Becky Sue's watery grave was.

I don't know how long I laid on that floor. The sun

gave way to the moon that peeked over the treetops. Crickets and katydids sang full tilt all around me. A single candle burned on the porch rail. I must'a lit it. But for the life of me, I had no recollection of doing so.

Visions are tricky things. Mine come out-of-the-blue. Some were sharp and clear while others were blurred and dull as a butter knife. Same way with haints. And while I was no stranger to seeing ghostly forms and certainly not feared of them, seeing a spirit appear right in front of my eyes still made me gasp. The misty figure standing a few feet from the cabin made me suck in a deep breath for sure.

There be something familiar about this ghost. Couldn't put my finger on it though. Couldn't make out its face neither, but I knew the haint had come for me. Without a second thought I bolted down the porch steps but stopped half way. Something was different. I turned back. The candle twinkled. My body still lay stretched out flat on the hard wood. Was I dead?

The cold, light touch of a ghostly hand on my shoulder made me jump a country mile and told me I was quite alive. I just didn't have the weight of my body to slow me down. This beat the sap out of changing into a crow or jaguar. Soul Walking. Who would've guessed? Wonder how I got out of my body? Don't remember doing nothing special. Didn't have no idea how I was going to get back into my skin neither, but I'd worry about that later. Right now I had to catch up with the bobbing, pale-yellow figure that wove through the mist. I reckon'd we'd gone a few miles before it dawned on me where we was headed. Fanes Creek.

Fanes Creek switched and twitched like an angry cat's tail around hollowed-out trees and thick brush.

Legend had it that Maribel Fane threw herself into the deepest part and drowned after her sweet William up and runned off with her younger sister. Maribel's tormented soul kept the current in constant uproar, and her lonely wail could be heard long before the churning water came into view. Folks didn't fish much or swim in Fanes Creek— too dark and gloomy. Besides the water stunk like rotten eggs.

I stopped at the stream's crusted edge and watched the haint float out into the middle of the creek. Inches above the roiling water, the figure hung eerie and silent in the air. I could see no expression on the phantom's blank face, but I got its message.

A fearsome sadness shook my bones when I fixed my gaze on the spirit. I knew right then there Hanna and Becky Sue rotted on the creek bottom.

The haint sunk beneath the dark surface.

Maribel Fane wasn't alone anymore.

Chapter 29

I flew into town. At Dixon's Feed Store, I shook loose from my sleek feathers and walked down Main, bold as brass. Some folks stared and gasped, no doubt thinking Bethany Ann Wayne done rose from the dead. Others didn't give me a second glance. It was bad timing on my part. Wesley and Wilkes were in the sheriff's office when I walked in.

"I know where they are."

Tate choked on his wad of gum. Benjamin leaped from his chair.

Funny how five little words can cause such a big ruckus. Mr. Wilkes said he had a good row boat and he and Mr. Wesley damn near broke down the door rushing out to fetch it. Nobody said nothing to me after I'd said Fanes Creek. On his way out, Benjamin finally stopped and looked at me.

I nodded back. "I'll meet you there."

A slight smile was his answer. He knew I could make better time as the crow flies.

I stood on the muddy shore and watched John Wesley and Harvey Wilkes row out to the middle of Fanes Creek. Sheriff Tate had come within a frog's hair of dropping to his knees and begging the two men to stay put at his office. But in the end he'd given in. After all, it was hard enough to deny one father's plea to go collect his daughter's remains. But two?

Benjamin and Tate waited a few yards downstream. The sheriff stood solid as stone. Benjamin, on the other hand, walked the creek bank. Every once in a while he'd stop, gaze out at the water, then shoot me a glance.

When the boat started back, Benjamin and the sheriff waded knee deep out into the murky water and helped drag it to shore. No one said nothing when Wesley and Wilkes lifted and placed two small bodies on the cold ground. I turned to go.

I done found Hanna and Becky Sue. Done released them from the water and scum. Nothing else left for me to do. When a third body was hauled from the boat, my heart skipped a beat. Benjamin asked the question stuck in everyone's craw.

"Buford? Anyone else report a girl missing?"

John Wesley cleared his throat. "Don't know who this one be, Sheriff Tate. But I wasn't about to leave her down there. No sir. Wasn't about to do that."

Tate heaved a sigh so deep it musta' shook his boots.

"I'll do it, Buford." Benjamin's voice came low but strong.

Takes a special kind of man to do folk's dirty work, but that don't mean he wouldn't regret it later. I'd seen the chewed on faces and blank eyes of the dead girls and even in a vision it were an ugly sight. I stepped toward Benjamin and threw an ounce of courage his way.

"You recognize her, Ben?"

"No. Never seen her before. Wait a minute. She's got something around her neck."

"Let me see," Tate said. "Might help identify her."

"Doubt it." The necklace dangled from his hand. "It's just a strip of old leather. What's that tied on the end?"

The sheriff's brow wrinkled. "Looks like a bobcat claw."

Feathers. Talons.

Growls. Snarls.

Claws. Fangs.

Ripping and tearing at my innards the crow and jaguar struggled to break free.

The third body laying naked, wet, and broken in the mud and muck was Sarah Rose.

Chapter 30

My body shook. Hot then cold chills raced up my back. My innards turned upside down and inside out. The jaguar and crow took turns rising to the surface. Weren't nothing I could do to stop them. Then again, I had no wish to keep them hid. In disbelief I stared at my best friend. A memory of a bright spring morning so long past flashed like lightning.

Folks in town labeled Sarah Rose's mama peculiar. Most kids didn't know what that word meant. They simply called her crazy. Sarah Rose never got angry or upset over this. For the life of me, I couldn't figure out why. Anybody call Mama loony, I'd clean their plow.

"Bethany Ann." Sarah Rose had said. "I know mama ain't crazy. She's just wore out."

Sarah Rose had wiped her hands on her sister's hand-me-down jeans and gave me a sad smile. "You know that old saying. 'God won't give you more than what you can handle?' Well, I don't hold to that notion. Sometimes Bethany Ann, life whittles a body down to a nub. No matter how hard ya' try, how good ya' be, there comes a time when ya' just can't take no more of being knocked down. Life has done sucked the will out of mama. She's lost faith and all hope. She ain't crazy, Bethany Ann, she just be at her wit's end. She can't take no more."

I never really understood what Sarah Rose had been

155

getting at until now. Seeing her body laying there all dark and hollow was my last straw.

Benjamin reached for me. The jaguar broke free. Fingers turned to claws. I swiped his arm.

"Get away!" I spat.

He jumped back a foot. Gawked goofy like at his torn shirt. Sheriff Tate, eyes round as dinner plates, eased up beside him. "Jesus, God, Ben. If I hadn't seen it with my own eyes, I'd never believed it. Doubt I'll ever sleep sound again." He glanced back at the boat.

"Get her under control, son. And quick. I can't have Wesley and Wilkes seeing her turning into a black panther to a crow back to a girl again right in front of their eyes. We got us enough trouble. Don't need those two whipping up panic, spreading the word all over town that Wayne's daughter is a wild-haired witchy woman. Folks be wanting to burn her at the stake for sure."

The hair on the back of my neck bristled and a low growl rumbled in my throat.

Benjamin turned and shoved the sheriff backwards. "Go away, Buford."

The wind kicked into high gear. The sun ran away and hid. Benjamin pushed Tate again. "Get those men out of here. Now! So far they've been too busy covering their daughter's bodies to pay any attention to what's been going on over here. Take them up the draw away from this side of the creek." Another shove. "Git!"

Never saw Tate waddle so fast.

Thunder boomed. Benjamin cringed. I pointed toward Sarah Rose.

"That be my best friend laying there, Benjamin. My best friend! And I killed her. It's all my fault!"

"For God's sake, Bethany Ann. Stop screaming. I

don't understand."

"And you think I do? I tried, Benjamin. Tried hard to keep her safe. How stupid. How very stupid of me. Thinking a strip of dried up cowhide and a sharp toenail could keep anyone from harm."

Head pounding, I paced the creek bed. Back and forth.

Feet turned to paws-to claws-to feet again.

Feathers-to fur-to-skin.

"I failed. Failed to save her when we was kids. Failed to protect her all grown up."

"Bethany Ann that's not true. You're…"

"I'm what, Benjamin? Tell me. What am I?" I shouted even louder. "A daughter of the Howling Moon? What a bunch of hogwash. Who am I foolin'? I ain't nothing. No big, powerful soldier against evil. No righteous fighter for truth. Nothing! I'm just flesh and blood. Like everyone else. I never ask for The Shimmering. Never asked to be some big protector of the innocent. I can't do this anymore, Benjamin. This never ending struggle against good and evil is too much for me."

Clouds broke and rain beat the ground.

"What's the use? Let the devil win. Let him plunge the world into darkness."

I glanced once more at Sarah Rose. Sadness swallowed me whole. My voice broke.

"It just don't matter no more."

Chapter 31

Ben had seen many sides of Bethany Ann but never defeat and that scared him. He had come to depend on her down-to-earth, homespun logic. Counted on the way she found the truth in all things. And, yes, even though it was hard for him to admit, her unshakable belief that good would always win had rekindled his hope and faith.

She was his rock. His salvation.

Seeing her standing there devoid of all hope drenched by the very rain her despair and sorrow had conjured, wrenched his heart. He'd seen this before in the war. Well, not the rapid shape shifting of course but certainly the loss of control. Soldiers sick and tired of the killing, torment, and everyday stress of just staying alive would crack under the pressure. Overwhelmed by the carnage and being stretched to their limits, they'd shut down. Some never rebounded. He wasn't about to let this happen to Bethany Ann. Not if he could help it.

He rubbed his arm. She'd attacked him once. Would she again? One cautious step after another he moved toward her until he was close enough to reach out and grab her. In one quick move, he crushed her to his chest. He saw Buford, Wesley and Wilkes trudging up the hill, each with a small body in their arms. Buford stopped at the top and looked back. Benjamin waved him on.

He didn't know how long he stood holding her in the rain. Finally he whispered, "Come on, let's go home."

She stirred. "Home? Ain't got no home, Benjamin." He heard her draw a ragged breath. "No home. No Mama. No best friend. No nothing."

"You're wrong, Bethany Ann."

The rain stopped. Sunlight struggled to break an opening through the clouds. He lifted her into his arms and carried her back to the jeep. Slumped against the passenger's window, eyes closed, she said nothing for about a mile. Then she turned toward him. The tears streaming down her cheeks tore his heart in half. .

"Just what do I have, Benjamin?"

His knuckles tightened on the steering wheel. His voice came low.

"Me, Bethany Ann. You've always got me."

Chapter 32

Ben shuffled through the door, twirled a chair around backwards, and sank onto to it. Buford glanced up from his newspaper. "Whoo-wee, son. You look like you've been rode hard and put up wet." He poured a cup of coffee from his thermos and slid it across the desk. "Any progress with the girl?"

"Nope. It's been over a week and she's still lifeless. Thought for sure she'd snap out it by now. All she does is sleep. Looks like an empty husk lying in the bed. All the life and light just went out of her."

"She's grieving, son."

"I don't understand. She didn't act this upset when her mother died."

"Ben, you know what your problem is with that girl?"

"Didn't know I had one."

"Well, I'm here to tell ya, you do. You've placed her so high up on a pedestal it's a wonder she don't have nose bleeds. Oh, I know she can do wondrous things but..."

"You don't know half of what she can do."

"And I don't want to either. I sleep better that way. What I'm trying to say is despite all her powers and abilities, she still only a half-grown woman who's lost everything. You got no idea what she did all alone in that swamp on those long summer nights after her mama died. She might'a bawled her eyes out for all ya know. Might'a cowered in fear every night waiting for Wayne to find her and finish what he started. She blames herself for Sarah Rose's death. Guilt can eat a hole plumb through your gut, son. Give her time, she'll come around. Stop thinking she's so high and mighty."

Ben's temper simmered. Bethany Ann had restored his faith. Returned hope to his heart. Buford would never understand the magnitude of this nor his relationship with Bethany Ann. Better to just change the subject. He cocked an eyebrow at the sheriff. "Hear from LeRoy yet?"

"Sure did, I was getting to that. LeRoy and Wayne's brother, Ezekiel paired up at a coon hunt last weekend. He flat out asked ol' Zeke why he hated his family."

"That took nerve."

The sheriff chuckled. "Well, ya gotta' understand. Both of them were two sheets to the wind. Suspect it was more shine than guts."

"Are Hester and Jedidiah brother and sister?"

"Yep."

"Oh God."

The sheriff stuck a piece of Juicy Fruit in his mouth. "Zeke called them fornicators. Told LeRoy he walked in once and found Hester in bed with Jed, arms and legs wrapped round him like a spider monkey hanging on to a coconut tree. That's when he disowned the whole bunch."

Sick to his stomach, Ben pushed the coffee cup away.

"Zeke also said Hester has a jealous streak a mile long. Hated any gal Wayne got tangled up with. He said when Jedidiah got a young woman with child and wanted

161

to marry her, Hester threw such a hissy fit, he moved away. Zeke heard the baby was a little girl."

Ben struggled for a breath. Danni. The baby girl was Danni.

"Zeke said he was surprised when Wayne didn't move back home after the girl's mama died in a car crash. Then he found out he'd hooked up with another woman."

Tate stared Ben right in the eye. "That be your mama, I suppose?"

Ben nodded but said nothing.

"Reckon you know the rest of the story. No need repeating it."

"No." Ben whispered. "No need for that."

"Zeke went on to say Jedidiah has a dirty sickness."

"Like sleeping with his sister isn't?"

"Zeke blames Hester for all of that. He said she poisoned Jedidiah's mind. Made him think she was the only who loved him. No, what Zeke was referring to was Wayne's fondness for little girls."

"Zeke knows about that?"

Buford ran his hands through thinning hair and sighed deep. "Suspects more than knows. He ain't never seen anything."

"So we're back to square one. We know Wayne is guilty, but all our proof is circumstantial."

"That about sums it up. I was hoping finding the girls would help. That they'd be some kind of evidence tying Wayne to them. But that wasn't the case. To add to insult to injury, Wesley and Wilkes are saying their girls drown accidental."

Ben's eyes widened. "In Fanes Creek? Nobody swims there. Besides they were naked."

"They said the rough current tore their clothes off."

"Are they blind or just stupid?"

"Now, Ben. Don't be so hard on them. No parent wants to think their young'un died from foul play. That they failed to protect them. It's much easier to come to terms with their death saying it was an accident or God's will."

Ben pushed back from the chair and walked from one end of the room to the other. "Then what are we going to do, boss? Wayne's gonna keep raping and killing unless we stop him. But how? Without proof we're just chasing our tails."

"Well, that brings up another interesting point I want to talk about."

Ben stopped in mid stride. "Which is?"

"Damn it, Ben, sit down. Your pacing like a caged lion grates my nerves."

He never thought anything could get under Buford's thick skin. This case had both of them on edge. He sat back down and waited for Buford to continue.

"When I contacted the Natchez police and told them about Sarah Rose they knew exactly who I was talking about. They said she worked as a waitress at a local café. When they informed her mama, she told them Sarah Rose was saving up every slap nickel and dime she made for a bus ticket to come visit her friend Bethany Ann."

"So."

"It was a surprise, Ben. No one knew she was coming into town."

"Then how did Wayne find her?"

"Excellent question. I asked myself the same thing."

Ben grinned. "Come up with an answer?"

"As a matter of fact, I did. I done some checking

around town. Found out the day the bus came in from Natchez with Sarah Rose on board, Hester Wayne was at Baker's Emporium looking at dress material."

"The bus station is across the street from Baker's."

"Yep. Hester saw Sarah Rose get off that bus."

"And she told Wayne."

Buford leaned back in his chair. "Maybe. Maybe not."

"Boss?"

"Ben, I don't doubt one minute Wayne ain't kidnapping those girls and having his way with them. The sick bastard. But. I wonder if he's the one killing them."

"You think it's Hester?"

"Could be. If she's as jealous as Zeke says, it makes perfect sense."

"Wouldn't he miss seeing them around town?"

Buford leaned back in the chair. "Not necessarily. Sarah Rose moved away few years back, so he wouldn't be looking for her."

"What about Hanna and Rebecca Sue?"

"They hadn't been gone all that long, besides it'd be just like Hester to tell him some long winded story about them being away. Doubt Wayne would it much thought anyways. His mind be working on what new girl he could grab."

Ben winced. His gut twisted and turned. Was there no way of proving Wayne's guilt? Frustration, too many sleepless nights on a too short couch, and worry over Bethany Ann showed in his voice. "Boss, how are we gonna stop this monster?"

Tate stood, reached up, and pulled the chain on the ceiling fan. He cleared his throat. "That brings up another problem I need to talk about."

Another problem? What could be worse than this? Ben glanced at the sheriff. Something was eating at the big man.

"Ok, boss. Spit it out. What's bothering you?"

"Bethany Ann."

"Bethany Ann? I don't understand."

The whop-whop of the fan blades shuffled the newspaper on Buford's Desk. The sheriff sat back down, folded the paper, and met Ben's gaze.

"Ben, I know how fond you are of that gal."

Not this again. His temper broke. "Damn it Buford. I told you a thousand times I don't have any romantic feelings for her. But if I did, why would that be any concern of yours?

"Now don't get your hackles up, boy. I ain't saying you're in love with her. Although from where I sit, I wouldn't blame ya none if ya were. No. What I'm getting at is this. Pretty soon that gal's sorrow and depression is gonna' turn into rip-snorting rage and when it does, she'll make a bee-line straight for Wayne. We've both seen firsthand what she's capable of doing when she's a little pissy. Can you image what she can do when she's really riled up?"

"She'll tear Wayne apart. Limb-by-limb"

"Yep and lick the blood off her chops when she's done. But that ain't what worries me."

Well, if Bethany Ann slaughtering Wayne in cold blood wasn't the problem, then what the hell was? He stared hard at the lawman sitting across from him. "Then what does?"

"I ain't so sure I want to stop her."

Chapter 33

I had fallen into a deep pit with jagged rocks all around me. From the smelly, moldy bottom I saw daylight only a grown tree length above me. It'd be easy to climb out. Just put one foot on one rock at a time until I reached the top. Shoot, for that matter, I could fly out. I weren't trapped. I didn't have to stay here. Yet I had no desire to escape the dark.

Benjamin tried to pull me up from the deep hole. Every day he'd show me another small wonder of his house. Water with only a turn of a round knob. Light with a flick of a switch. Coffee from a pot plugged into the wall. Oh, and best of all, an inside bathroom with a washtub and a special contraption that rained buckets of hot water down my neck and back. Soap that didn't strip the hide plumb off ya. Flowery smelling stuff to wash my hair with.

I must've worried him something fierce. I'd see him sigh when I only nibbled at the melted cheese sandwich and sipped the tomato soup, he bragged was his specialty. It weren't that the food wasn't tasty, it was just too much trouble to chew and swallow. His square jaw clenched when I'd pushed away from the shiny steel table to curl into his soft bed and fall into the void. The well. The pit.

"Talk to me." He musta' said that a hundred times.

"Can't," was always my answer.

"It isn't your fault. You didn't kill her."

That's what he thought. I knew better.

He never lost patience. Never pushed me. For that kindness, I'd always be beholding to him. Even though I wanted to ease his mind, I had no will to take up my bed and walk.

But all that changed the morning Sarah Rose showed up.

She stood at the foot of the bed, hands on her small hips, glaring down at me. "I got a bone to pick with you."

"What?"

"Ain't you sick of wallowing around in sorrow and pity?"

"I got every right to waller," I shot back at her. "It's my fault you're dead, ya know."

"Oh, Bethany Ann, what a bunch of hooey."

Never heard the bite so strong in her tiny voice before. I gawked at her.

"Quit staring at me like a big-eyed hooty owl. I heared what you said back there at the creek. Heared you say let the devil have it all. What the Sam Hill is wrong with you? That ain't the Bethany Ann I know."

"I'm tired. I—

"Hush up!"

Whoa! Never, ever heard her talk that way before. What was it with Death? The Grim Reaper done gave Mama a backbone before she crossed and had filled my best friend with piss and vinegar. Maybe Death stripped away all pretending and left a person free to be who they really was. Too bad so many folks had to die before they found that kind of courage.

"Angels don't talk like that, Sarah Rose."

"They do when they hear the hogwash you been

spewing. Besides I ain't no angel. Not yet anyways. I ain't crossed. Which is why I'm standing here now. I'm trapped between worlds until you avenge my death and set my soul free. Same with Hanna and Becky Sue."

"Don't put that burden on me, Sarah Rose."

"Burden?

Never knew haints could get so red in the face.

"You best listen to me, Bethany Ann, and listen good. You are the daughter of the Howling Moon. Your God-given purpose for living is to fight evil. It's your duty to ease this so called burden of mine."

Good point.

"You're taller," I said.

"Don't change the subject."

I laughed. How strange. Sarah Rose was a haint yet she looked flesh and blood. We still talked like nothing had changed.

"It ain't fair, you being dead and all. You was supposed to grow up, get hitched to a beau with dreamboat eyes. Have a son named Ichabod. When I seen you there at the creek, all hollowed out like a punkin shell, no life, no light shining in those gooseberry eyes of yours, my heart done shriveled up and keeled over. Why did you have to die? Why?"

"Do you know how lucky you are?"

I stared a hole plumb through her which weren't too hard considin' she has half ghost.

What a stupid question to ask at a time like this. "Crying out loud, Sarah Rose, what kind of damned fool question is that?"

A small grin spread over her face. "Still swearing I see. Guess some things won't never change."

Again I laughed.

"So many folks question why they was born, Bethany Ann. Wonder what their purpose in life is. And they die never knowing. But you're lucky. You know. You was sent here to rain vengeance down upon those who try to destroy all that is good and holy in this world, to give hope to the weak, and justice to the wronged. You're God's warrior. Sent down from the heavens to fight for His good, His glory. They be very few people in this world special as you. If you don't stop evil in its tracks, who will?"

Sometimes it takes a good friend to whisper the truth before you can hear.

"Sarah Rose? Do you know what your purpose was? Why you was born?"

"To save you."

Didn't see that coming, damned near fell out of bed. Musta' looked like a silly goose cause this time she laughed.

"You forgot what a powerful trickster the devil is, Bethany Ann. How he studies a soul, finding out what weaknesses there be that he can twist and turn to his favor. You're hot on his forked tail. He needed you to stop. So he kilt me. He knew my death would be the one thing that would push you over the edge. Make you lose faith. Make you too weak to fight both him and the guilt he piled up in your heart. Good plan. It almost worked too…except."

"Except what?"

"Except he didn't count on how strong love for a friend can be. So strong death can't even destroy it." The little sob in her voice made my heart ache. "You will always be my best friend."

"You're always be mine too."

She ducked her head and drew a deep breath. Kinda of funny seeing a sigh so deep from a ghost. Guess it was because she hadn't fully crossed yet.

"I never told you, but Mama and Daddy fought like a couple of pit bulls, what with his drinking and whoring around and her bitterness and hate. I couldn't count on my folks for nothin'. And when I needed Mama the most…when Jedidiah ruined me, she turned her back on me. She didn't give a hoot or a holler on how bad I hurt. How I needed someone to tell me it weren't my fault. Tell me he was all to blame."

I never knew haints could cry, neither.

"But I could always depend on you, Bethany Ann. You was the one who hugged and cried with me. You held my hand at meeting, even stepped between me and Jedidiah when he got that lusting glare in his eyes. You cared. So much so you made a necklace out of leather and claws so I'd be protected."

"That stupid little trinket didn't save you one bit, Sarah Rose."

"Don't call it stupid!" She rolled her eyes at me. "Sometimes for all your witchy woman ways, you're thicker than tree sap. It weren't the actual object, but the love and compassion, the intent you put into every twist of that leather that rescued me from falling into darkness."

Shoot fire. Now I was tearing up.

"You never ignored me Bethany Ann. And I ain't about to leave you in your hour of need neither." She drew a deep breath. "Get this straight. You did not kill me." Her voice turned to granite. "But we both know who did.

"Jedidiah haunted my dreams, ya know. Moving

170

away did nothing to stop the nightmares. He'd sneak into my room at night. I could still feel his hands pawing and groping. Smell his puke breath. Taste his spit on my lips. But when I woke up covered in a cold sweat and sick to my belly, I'd clutch your necklace to my heart and remember your vow."

I didn't dare move an inch. Never seen her so fierce.

"You promised me, Bethany Ann. Promised years ago you'd kill Jedidiah for what he did to me and the others. Knowing somehow, someday you'd make him pay for what he done gave me the strength to keep going on. Kept me believing in that good you're always preaching about and fighting for."

The look she shot me sent chills skittering all over my body.

"The law won't never find a way to stop Jedidiah. You're the only one who can destroy him and the evil that walks beside him. Don't you dare let him win, Bethany Ann. Don't you dare. Don't let my death be for nothing."

She reached for me.

"Now get up!"

I grabbed her hand and clawed my way up into the light once more.

Chapter 34

The stench of sulfur fumes jarred Ben from deep sleep. Fire burned all around. Burned, but did not consume. Coughing. Sputtering. Lungs begged for a taste of fresh, crisp air. None was to be found in the smothering heat and stink. He stepped out of bed. And fell.

Down.

Down.

Down.

Down into a pit of rotting flesh. Broken skulls. Brittle bones under foot. Snap and crunch with every step.

"Benjamin, where are you?"

Danni? His heart slammed against his breastbone.

"Benjamin. Help me."

It *was* Danni. Where? Eyes burned. Wouldn't focus. "Danni?"

"Benjamin. Help me."

Christ, where the hell was he? His breath caught. Hell? Oh God. He was in hell. Wait. Danni wouldn't be in hell. Or would she? People who commit suicide burn for all eternity. Wasn't that what the Church said? No. Not Danni. She was the definition of innocence and goodness. This wasn't right. He was dreaming. Yeah. That's what it was.

A dream. A nightmare.

All he had to do was open his eyes.

He struggled. Fought to wake. But smoke and ash stood firm. No blanket, pillow or morning light came to his rescue.

"Ben-ja-min!"

His name screamed in pain and torture made him cringe. *Find Dann!. Help her!*

He groped his way through shadows. Stagnant, foul air made his head spin. He clasped a hand over his nose and mouth to block the fetid odor. An orange pinprick of light pierced the dark. A campfire. A caldron. Chanting. A voodoo ceremony? Was he in the swamps? How? Had he been drugged?

He stumbled into the clearing.

Ghostly figures gathered around the fire turned as one. Little girls. Young girls with long, blonde hair every one of them. Wide, oversized green eyes distorted their pasty-white faces. Tiny bony fingers stripped of all flesh beckoned him closer. Pointed to the boiling kettle.

No. He didn't want to look. Wouldn't look.

"Benjamin."

This time his name came whisper soft. Bewitching as sirens, the voices beckoned him closer.

Powerless to resist, he gazed into the blacken pot.

Buford Tate's severed head bobbed in the churning water.

Hideous, grotesque laughter spewed from the girls decayed mouths.

Ben crumbled to his knees. Covered his ears to drown out the sound.

It's just a dream. Wake up. For the love of God. Wake up!

The ground crawled toward him. Scratching sounds

rose from beneath the dirt. Cockroaches. Hundreds of them. Horrified, he sat stunned. The vile insects marched closer. Long and brown like Roi-Tan cigars only with legs…and wings. They covered his boots. Scurried up his pant legs.

Move!

He jumped to his feet. Beat at his legs. Stomped his boots. Filthy, crusty bodies crunched like ginger snaps under the heavy soles. Ben gagged.

He ran.

Swatted at the flying bugs surrounding him. Fought down bile at the sickening thud when one slammed into his head.

He ran.

This was no dream. A nightmare, yes. But no dream. He could wake from a mere dream, forget it, and be done. But this night terror wouldn't yield to daylight. His eyes refused to open. He had to be drugged. Hallucinating. It was the only explanation. But who would've done such a thing? And why?

He ran.

God, he hated the disgusting swamp. Damn wetlands scrambled his head. Robbed him of his nerve and common sense. Always black as pitch, full of twisted, deformed trees, wearing sinister faces of wood and moss with long narrow branches reaching like human fingers to grope and tear at his clothes. Bottomless bogs that could swallow him whole never to be seen again. Gators that'd chewed and chomped. Spirit of the swamps his ass.

War had been hell. But at least the enemy was flesh and bone, mortal men he recognized and understood. But in the swamps he never knew what phantom wickedness lurked ahead, behind, or beside him. Bethany Ann was right. How could he defend himself against a foe he could neither see nor touch? How could he kill evil?

Exhausted, he tripped and fell.

Face down in the stinking moist and moldy swamp floor, he gasped for air. Tried to collect his wits.

A rustling in the bushes a few feet from his head made him raise his gaze.

Glowing red eyes peered out from the brush. Ben's blood turned to ice. Shit. Ghosts, severed heads, flying cockroaches. What now? He scrambled to his feet.

The beast stomped toward him and raised its hideous head. Ben took a step back. What sort of hellish creature towered over him? A head full of spikes and horns, beady eyes, a split tongue that flicked back and forth, a massive leathery body and razor claws the size of butcher knives.

"Benjamin, help me." Wicked, taunting laughter spewed from the monster's mouth.

Ben gasped. This was the voice that pulled him deeper into the dark, not Danni's. What was wrong with him? He should've known. Danni always called him Bennie, never Benjamin. He took another step back and reached for his revolver. Damn! His holster was empty. Yet another piece of evidence that proved he was seeing things. He never went into the swamps without his .357. Not that the gun would've helped. He'd need a cannon to blow the head of this scaly bastard.

The dragon came closer. Ben stepped backwards. His heart flipped over and froze when his back hit the cypress tree. Trapped. No place to run. Lightning fast the creature raked sharp claws across Ben's arm.

The excruciating pain threw him to his knees. Liquid

fire raced up his wrist to his elbow, and burned like acid. Each throb of his pulse twisted his heart. His arm hung limp. Useless. Could he die from a hallucination?

The beast moved within a foot of Ben. The stench of decay and death covered him like a shroud. So this was how he would die? He'd survived the trenches of Germany only to be mauled to death in the muck and filth of the Louisiana swamps? Ripped to pieces by a demon beast neither human nor animal? Was this his punishment for doubting the Word of God? To be killed by the Beast of Revelation?

The monster hissed, "We kill rabid animals around these here parts."

In a flash Bethany Ann's words came back to him. "Evil can twist and turn and slip through cracks, Benjamin, and never plays fair." Now he understood. This was no flesh and blood creature but the evil entity of Jedidiah Wayne hovering above him. Closing in for the kill.

Again razorblade claws reached out. Torn to shreds, Ben's shirt fell to the ground. A screech split the air. Ben clutched his arm and watched the creature back away. Why? He glanced down.

The gris-gris bag hung around his neck. He'd worn it ever since that first day he and Buford had talked to Wayne. He didn't really believe the charm had power, but like the sheriff said, there was no harm in being prepared. Well, he damned sure believed now.

The monster's spiked head swayed back and forth. Forked tongue flicked. The gris-gris bag may have temporarily stalled the attack, but would it be enough to save him?

Funny how your mind works when facing death. Ben

reasoned that no matter the excuse for killing, in the end, it all boiled down to one thing. Good versus evil. Which one was the most powerful?

The beast rushed forward.

Ben did the only thing he knew to save himself.

He cried out to the angels.

Chapter 35

I heard his call in my sleep.

Benjamin was a non-believer. He musta' been in one hell of a fix to cry out to God for help. I knew that feeling. The helplessness and fear. Where was he? I brought his face to mind, reached out, and caught his being. Blackness all around. Fire and sulfur. His soul was trapped in the land between the livin' and the dead.

Evil ruled this shadow land always looking for unaware souls to drag into its foulness. I'd warned Benjamin that Jedidiah had marked him. To be alert. But now weren't the time to be thinking, "I told ya so." A soul taken in that in-between realm was doomed to wander lost and alone through eternity. Didn't have no choice but to go in after him. But not as a human.

I'd have to be the jungle cat.

Jaguars were ruled by the moon and controlled the life and power of the night. I would need keen eyesight to pierce the darkness, swiftness and cunning to outsmart Evil's tricks, strong jaws to crush the demon's hold, and fierceness to kill.

The itch in my belly turned into a fearsome scratch. Heat washed over me.

I turned the panther loose.

Chapter 36

A fierce yowl sliced the night.

A large, dark figure slinked from the wilds. Crouched low, the stealthy cat circled the tree, icy green eyes fixed on the dragon. Ears pinned flat against her head, long, white fangs bared, the jaguar stood between Ben and the beast. She growled.

As if hit by scalding water, the dragon recoiled from the jaguar's snarl. Was that fear Ben saw in those beady eyes? Time stopped. Soaked with sweat, he dared not move or breathe.

The demon lowered its ugly head and swung it from side-to-side looking for a weakness, an opening to strike. The jungle cat hugged the ground, hissed and spat. Her long tail switched back and forth. Waiting. Watching. Ready to pounce.

The demon struck.

The jaguar leapt from the ground. Rapier claws tore and ripped. Fangs plunged deep . Powerful jaws held tight. The demon screamed in pain. Blood poured, colored the dirt a rusty red and spattered against Ben's face.

Wide-eyed, heart pounding so hard he thought his ribs would shatter, Ben shouted when the fierce jungle cat took the beast to the ground. One last brutal shake and the demon lay dead.

The sleek cat shook her body, wrinkled her nose.

Rubbed her head and muzzle against bushes and course tree bark.

"Bethany Ann?"

Ben's whisper stopped her in mid-stride. She turned. For one long moment they stared into each other's eyes.

The jaguar melted into the dark and was gone.

Legs weak, Ben slid to the ground. The scent of blood, guts, and death sickened him. Rolling to his knees, he vomited. Violent heaves shook his body. Bare-chested, dripping with sweat, he shivered in the oppressive heat. Energy spent, dog-tired, he collapsed against the cypress and shut his eyes. A hissing sent jolts of adenine racing through his veins. Jesus Christ there was no way he could face another demon from hell. Fighting panic, he opened his eyes and braced himself for the worse. His gaze flew to the butchered monster.

Thunder rumbled. Lightning flashed.

The dragon vanished in a blaze of fire and smoke.

Chapter 37

Ben jerked awake.

Where was he? Faded wallpaper. One window facing west. He sniffed. No stench of fire and brimstone just a faint whiff of the trash he'd forgotten to take out. Thank God. Relieved, he sank back into the pillow and sighed deep. What a nightmare.

He uncurled from the couch and headed toward the bathroom careful not to wake Bethany Ann. He gazed down. Damn, Every muscle ached. His arm and hand hung numb. *Must be asleep, slept on it wrong.* Trying to get the feeling back, he flexed his fingers. Fire raced up his arm. He winced and shuffled into the bathroom and closed the door. Mouth tasted like day-old beer and stale cigarettes. He reached for his toothbrush, looked into the mirror, and froze.

Blood.

Dried blood on his face and chest. Deep scratch marks on his arm. He stood flat-footed and stupid, gawking at the image in the glass. What the hell? He started to shake. Jesus. God. Everything had really happened. The young girls. Buford's floating head. Flying cockroaches. The dragon. Everything. How?

Anger overrode shock.

Damn it!

He was sick to death of this mumbo-jumbo bullshit. Pissed at being jerked around by forces he didn't understand. He wanted answers. Now. No way would he wake Bethany Ann. But she wasn't the only person knowledgeable in the strange and unexplained.

He stood under the shower until the hot water turned cold. Feeling came back into his arm, pain tagged behind it. He struggled into his clothes, making sure the gris-gris bag still hung around his neck, buckled the .357 around his waist, and stormed out the door.

How the hell Lady Tibatha knew he was coming was beyond him. But there she was. Sitting on the front porch. Waiting. Dark eyebrows arched, and she led him into the cool kitchen without saying a word. A soothing light scent of lavender sweetened the air. Sylvester cat wove figure eights around his legs making it hard to walk.

"Him missed you," she said. "You sit."

Head spinning, he sank into the cushioned kitchen chair. He wasn't sure if the incense or the pain in his arm made him dizzy. Probably both. Back turned, Lady Tibatha busied herself at the small stove. Ben heard her humming. Soft and low. Sounded like a lullaby. She placed a cup in front of him. "Drink."

Sylvester leaped in his lap and pawed at the cup. Leery, Ben took a whiff of the minty smelling brew. Heart-shaped leaves floated on top. He rolled his eyes and looked at her. "What is this?"

"Catnip.

"You're kidding."

"Catnip calm de nerves and ease pain." Again, her brows lifted. "You hurt, don't you?"

His arm throbbed like a son-of-a-bitch, but how did she know?

He put the mug down and rolled up his shirt sleeve.

Black and yellow bruises surrounded the deep claw marks. "Got anything to put on these?"

Sylvester let out a yowl and dipped a curled paw into the cup. Ben fished-out a catnip flower. He smiled when the cat jumped down from the table and pranced away, tail-high, the leaf dangling from the side of his mouth.

Lady Tibatha sat beside him with a steaming bowl of water and a tiny brown bottle. She clicked her tongue and peered at him under long lashes. "These be the marks of the dragon," she said and cleaned the scratches. "Is that not so?"

"Yep, that's so," Ben said through clenched teeth.

She pushed the tea toward him. "Drink. Then tell me all."

Between sips he told the nightmare. She let him talk and said nothing while she dipped a corner of the washrag into the bottle. Feather soft, she applied oil to the marks. The burning stopped. "What sort of magic potion is that?" he asked

"Frankincense and myrrh."

"Isn't that what the wise men gave baby Jesus?"

A slight smile crossed her full lips. "I believe dat be the story. The oil good for healing. Soon no more pain, but not so the scars. They be with you forever." She pushed the bowl aside, took his cup, and refilled it.

"Well? he asked. "You gonna explain what happened last night?"

"It be no dream," she said. "As I say before, there be many dimensions unknown to the waking mind. Just because the body sleeps, it not mean the soul rests. You were marked by evil and tricked into the realm between the living and the dead."

"Why?"

"You threaten evil's power. It must destroy you. Many times evil comes in the form of the dragon." A slight cock of her head. "You know in this world who this evil be?"

"Oh yeah, I know."

"And the jaguar?"

He didn't answer . Didn't have to. She knew damn well the cat was Bethany Ann.

"Your bond with the panther is strong for her to hear your call throughout all dimensions."

He changed the subject. "Will the dragon come back?"

"Evil never gives up and will take many forms to trick you."

"How can I defeat it?"

"Only good can destroy evil."

He guessed the catnip tea and calming lavender had taken his edge off. Her trite answer should've aggravated him, but instead, he chuckled. "Gonna need a little more than that."

"In this waking world, evil can do you no harm because you stand firm in your belief of the law. But when in sleep, your soul wanders lost. There be no faith in a greater good to ground you. To destroy evil, you must believe in a power bigger than yourself."

"You mean God?"

"I mean Good. Name it what you wish."

Her hand reached for his. "Was it not your Christian savior who said if you have faith as small as a mustard seed, you can move mountains? Find your mustard seed, Benjamin Sol. Only then can you destroy the evil that stalks you."

She pushed away from the table and took the bowl

to the sink. Sylvester strolled back into the room. The cat plopped down in the sunlight that spilled across the wood floor and stretched. Ben laughed. "He's feeling no pain."

"And you? Your arm be better?"

Ben flexed his fingers. "Good as new."

She gave him a handful of crystals and a small pouch. "You take these. Put a crystal in the four corners of your house and in the windows." She opened the little bag. "Sprinkle a line of sea salt across your doorway."

Ben cocked an eyebrow. "This is supposed to keep me safe?"

"Do as I say, Benjamin Sol. Do not invite the devil in."

"Invite him in? I didn't exactly roll out the welcome mat for him the first time."

"But you did not tell him no, either. Now you be aware. Evil cannot enter where it not be welcomed."

What a bunch of bullshit. How could rocks and salt protect him against what he'd just seen? He ran his fingers over the scratch marks.

Then again, what could it hurt?

Chapter 38

Lightning bugs were out and about when Benjamin walked through the door. He grinned like a fat possum when he saw me sipping a Grape Nehi at the kitchen table. Guess it tickled him seeing me up and around instead of burrowed deep in the covers. He went to that fancy electric icebox of his and grabbed a pop. He sat across from me and took a deep gulp.

"I have to go, Benjamin."

His smile faded.

Long minutes ticked loud from his kitchen clock. The rustle of the breeze outside whistled around the windows. We sat and sipped awhile. He grinned again. "Stay."

"Can't, wouldn't be fittin'. We ain't hitched and we ain't kin. Folks are bound to talk."

"I don't care what people say." He cocked his head at me. "Didn't think you did either."

"I don't. But you're the deputy sheriff. You need their respect. Besides I got something I gotta' do."

I done ruined his smile again. He wiped the sweat trickling off the pop bottle on his pants leg and took a deep breath.

"Like what?"

"Kill Jedidiah Wayne."

He winced. "That's what I was afraid of." A big sigh. "I can't let you do that, Bethany Ann."

Like he could stop me.

"Benjamin —-"

His hand shot out and grabbed my wrist quicker than a duck on a June bug. "I mean it."

Ordinarily, I wouldn't paid too much mind to his grabbing my arm, but I weren't in a particularly forgivin' mood at that moment. I glared at his hand. He pulled back.

"I thought we was together on this, Benjamin. Don't ya think Jedidiah deserves to die for what he's done?"

"He deserves to be punished, yes. But it's up to the law to determine how."

"The *Law* has determined."

He snorted. "Who's law? Yours?"

The grimace on his face told me he knew he'd made a big mistake making fun of my belief in a higher power. Benjamin was my best friend. My split-in-half. He'd been there when I needed someone. I could never repay the kindness he's shown me. Even though his tone irked me, the last thing I wanted was to go leaving cross words between us.

I pushed back from the table and started toward the door. I should've kept on going. Should've paid no never mind to his smart-mouth remark. But ever since seeing Sarah Rose, my whole being had caught fire.

The Bible said it all. "To everything there is a season, and a time for every purpose under the heaven." Well the time for weeping and mourning was over. The time for killing was at hand. I weren't in no mood to have my actions called into question or justified. Hand on the doorknob, I paused and gazed back at him.

"Yes, Benjamin. Mine. I answer to a higher more fiercesome law than you will ever understand. A law older and wiser than any manmade rule that tin star pinned on your chest could ever stand for."

" 'Thou shalt not kill.' What about that rule?"

Didn't see that one coming. My temper flared.

"Well, listen to you, Mr. Non-Believer. Throwing the Good Book up in my face. Thought you'd turned your back on all that's holy. Thought you didn't believe no more."

"I believe in you."

His confession threw me for a loop. I stood rooted to the spot. Before I could think of anything to say he bolted from his chair and stood in front of my face.

"Bethany Ann, I've never known anyone so strong in the Faith as you. So dedicated to a higher, greater power. You've shown me good still exists and that it's worth fighting for. I may not believe one hundred percent, not yet, but you do, and that steadfast conviction has renewed my faith. You've saved me."

Being told I was his salvation was mighty powerful words. My head spun.

"I have no doubt you could kill Jedidiah Wayne with just a crook of your finger, but I'm begging you don't."

"Why?"

"If you can kill in cold blood, you're as evil as he is."

He took my hand from the doorknob and squeezed it.

"You're obsessed with Satan. Jedidiah Wayne is a flesh and blood man. Not the devil incarnate. Can't you see that? Killing Wayne will not destroy the devil. But it will destroy you…and me."

He could've been whistling Dixie for all I cared. I heard him yammering on, caught certain words here and there, but I weren't paying too much attention to him. I'd pretty much quit listening after he said I was no better than Jedidiah.

After everything we'd been through. After crossing over into different realms. Finding his mama, and her confessing Jedidiah done killed her. After saving his ass from the beast of Revelations. And by his own words, after saving his lost and tormented soul, he had the gall to say I was as low down and vile as Jedidiah Wayne?

I slapped him.

He dropped my hand. Jumped back like a scalded dog. Shock and confusion ran wild across his face.

"How dare you say that! I'll have you know that I'm tons better than Jedidiah Wayne and most folks that walk this earth. I don't rip the innocence plumb out of little girls for the pure fun of seeing the terror in their eyes and forcing screams from their mouths. I don't mock the Lord. Hide behind the collar, preaching God is Love, beating the Bible with one hand while groping and pawing young, tender flesh with the other.

"And I ain't no stupid county hick neither. Course I know Jedidiah Wayne and the devil ain't one in the same. Just like I know killing him won't end all the evil in the world, but he'll be one less demon I'll have to worry about."

"Bethany Ann, I'm sorry. I didn't mean…"

Too late to apologize. He done whupped me into a lather. Weren't interested in nothing he had to say. Maybe later, when I'd calmed down some, I'd understand his reasoning. But not now. Not yet. I lit into him again.

"But you were right about one thing. I do have a burning passion to wipe out all that is bad because I am the Daughter of the Howling Moon. A demon fighter. Conceived for the sole purpose of whupping the devil's ass. I bow before no man, including you."

He just stood there looking stupid. Didn't he know how hurtful his words were? Calling me obsessed. True, I weren't too sure of that word's meaning, but I sure as hell understood how he'd said it, and I didn't like it. Pissed me off to no end. I itched to slap him again. I gulped in a deep breath instead.

"I thought out of all the folks in the world you understood who I was. What I stood for. Guess I was wrong."

I jerked the door open.

"I'm going to do my God-given duty. Don't care if you like it or not. If that means you lose your way, your faith and hope all over again, then 'Work out your own salvation with fear and trembling.'"

"Bethany Ann!"

Again I turned back. The pleading in his blue eyes almost melted my anger. Almost made me sorry I'd slapped him. But then he opened his mouth and ruined it.

"You are so damn hard-headed. Do you know what you've just done? The kind of position you've put me in? You've just confessed to an officer of the law that you're going to commit cold-blooded, premeditated murder. I won't have a choice. I'll have to hunt you down. Arrest you. You might get life in prison. Doubt it. Killing a man of the cloth in cold blood will likely get you the electric chair. Do you understand what I'm saying? They'll execute you, Bethany Ann."

Still wanting him to hurt as bad as he done hurt me, I laughed in his face.

"Don't you fret none about that, Mr. High-and-Mighty Lawman. You ain't never gonna catch me."

I slammed the door in his face and flew off into the night.

Chapter 39

It took a while after flying back to the swamp and falling into my own skin again to start thinking straight. Bless Benjamin's heart. He was only trying to protect me. Being the die-hard lawman that he was, I'd be putting him between a rock and a hard place if I kilt in cold blood. He'd have to choose between the law and me. He'd pick me. Weren't no doubt about it. But I had no more right asking him to turn his back on the thing he believed in the most, than he did asking me to ignore who I was. The law was his destiny. His calling. Just like the Howling Moon was mine.

For Benjamin's sake I wouldn't kill Jedidiah without just cause. However, protecting myself was something else entirely. But Jedidiah was smart. He wouldn't attack me in the open. I'd have to figure out a way to goad him into coming after me and confess in front of his worshippers what evil he'd done. No need making him into some kind of sacrificial lamb in their eyes.

I sat on the porch steps and took in a deep breath of humid air. The scent of muddy water, wilting plants, and soggy dirt attacked my nose. Frog grunts, loon calls, and katydid hums filled my ears. It was good to be home. While it were true, I did like Benjamin's fancy inside washtub and lights with a flip of a switch, his place would never give me the peace of mind this two-room shack surrounded by wood and water always did. These wilds was my sanctuary. My refuge. My church.

No doubt most folks would think I was touched in the head for thinking a tiny cabin deep in the swamp could be a church, but to my way of thinking, it made perfect sense. A place of worship didn't have to be no big fancy building with stained glass in the windows and a steeple tall enough to touch the floor of heaven. Church was any place you could find peace, and quiet both the body and soul. Talk to God like He was sitting across the kitchen table sharing morning coffee with ya.

Church should also be a blessed, safe place. Jedidiah done took advantage of that notion. He'd turned a sacred house of God into a snake hole full of torment and ruin. There was only one sure way I knew of to destroy a viper pit.

Burn it.

Chapter 40

Ben sat at the kitchen table and stared out the window. Twilight faded to black. Half of the moon's bald head poked over the horizon. Wouldn't be too long now, maybe thirty minutes or so, until its whole face would stand bold in the inky sky. A full moon night. He smiled. Bethany Ann's kind of night. His lips straighten into a hard line.

For over a week he'd watched despair eat the life right out of her. He'd feared the girl with the crescent moon in her eyes and fire in her blood would be lost forever. He'd wished with all his being she would return. Seeing her at the table earlier that evening, devoid of all depression and full of fight once more, made him want to shout with joy.

His hand smacked the table hard. The Nehi bottle rolled and hit the floor. Damn it! He'd ruined everything.

He should've kept his big mouth shut. But she'd been so. . . so…cocky. Without batting an eyelash, she'd declared her murderous intent. To him. A deputy sheriff. Cool and calm. Like killing another human being was nothing out of the ordinary. Nothing to worry about. Good God. Buford was right. Grief had turned to ice-cold vengeance.

He pushed his chair back and picked up the pop bottle. How typical. He'd wished for the old Bethany Ann to return and she had. Full bore. A dry, humorous chuckle broke the silence in the room. *Be careful what you wish for, Benjamin.*

He was only trying to warn her. But his words had come out all wrong. Damn it. If she killed Jedidiah in cold blood the town would crucify her. He couldn't…wouldn't let that happen. He'd refuse to track her down. The law be damned. And she knew it.

He'd never find her in that swamp anyway. She could turn into a crow, gator, snake, or a fucking blade of grass if she wanted. And she knew it.

She had power and dominion over everything that breathed in that wetland as well as some things that didn't draw breath. The wilds loved her. Hated him. And she knew it.

A loud knock made him jump. Bethany Ann? He opened the door a crack. Buford Tate pushed into the room.

"Buckle on that cannon of yours, boy, and let's get moving."

He fastened his gun belt. A million questions spilled from his mouth. "Boss? What the hell? What's going on? Go where?"

Buford grabbed him by the shirt collar and pulled him outside. "Listen to that, son. Every dad-blasted dawg in this here town has gone stark raving mad. Howling like there ain't gonna be no tomorrow."

It was true. Sounded like packs of wolves roamed the streets. The hair on Ben's neck bristled. "What's got them so riled up?"

The sheriff pointed at the sky.

Every ounce of air flew from his lungs in one big gasp. Never had he seen the moon so huge. Streaks of orange, purple, and red moved across its face. Like

God's omniscient eyeball hanging in the darkness, watching, waiting.

Buford pulled at his shirt again. "Ben, Tibby just left my office. She had a vision. We got to get over to Wayne's church, fast."

Unable to resist the moon's mysterious pull, Ben stood solid. "Look at it, boss. Damn thing's so close looks like we could touch it. Ever see clouds so dark and threatening?

"Tibby called it a bad moon rising. Ben, we gotta git!"

He stumbled towards the White Rose. "Why? What's fixing to happen?"

Sheriff Tate swallowed hard. "Tibby had a name for that kind of moon, Ben."

"Which is?"

"A Howling Moon."

His blood turned to ice. *Bethany Ann's moon.*

Buford slid behind the wheel. "Tibby said something else tonight, too."

The tremor in Buford's voice made his knees weak. He sank hard into the passenger's seat. He didn't want to know. Didn't want to ask. He had no choice. "What was that?"

"The battle between good and evil has begun."

Chapter 41

Ben's head swam with air so thick and heavy a sharp knife could slice it into bite-size chunks. Beside him, Buford sweated bullets. They'd waited at the church for over an hour and still no sign of Bethany Ann.

"Boss, maybe Lady Tibatha had it all wrong. Maybe it wasn't Wayne's church she saw burned to the ground."

"Well, you tell me, son. You've sat across the table from Tibby a few times. Think she'd make a mistake about something as big as this?"

Annoyed, Ben didn't bother to answer. He slapped at the mosquitoes buzzing around his head and stamped his boots. He'd been standing in one place too long. Legs felt like tree trunks. He needed to move. To pace.

Movement caught the corner of his eye.

Crouched low, a large black shadow hugged the tree line. His jaw tightened. Should've figured Bethany Ann would check things out as the jungle cat first.

The panther hesitated. Ears pricked. Nose sniffed the air. She moved on. Padded into the clearing.

Silent. Alert.

A silk shadow in the moon's glow.

An icy green stare thrown his way made Ben grimace.

A switch of her long tail.

Busted. The sleek cat knew they hid among the cypress. She turned her back on them, unconcerned. Bad

197

sign. She was focused on only one thing. The church before her.

Lights flickered in every window. Shouts of hallelujahs and amens echoed out into the star-infested night. Wednesday night meeting. Ben shook his head. No. Surely to God, Bethany Ann wouldn't burn the place with people in it. He heard a low growl rumble deep in the cat's throat. Or would she?

He glanced over at Buford then turned back. Only for a second. But in that splinter of time the panther leaped back into human skin. Bethany Ann stood in the cat's prints.

He wanted to shout out a warning. Wanted to pull her away. But he couldn't. The stunned look on Buford's face told him the sheriff's movements were frozen as well. Some unknown force held them captive. Damn. With one green stare, she'd cast a spell over them. He had to hand it to her. She'd made it more than plain. Neither he nor Buford were to interfere in the events of this night. Helpless, all they could do was wait. And watch.

The spell started with a whisper.

Gliding over the treetops, the moon cast its brilliance to the ground. The scrape of a circle being scratched into dirt echoed in the silence. Arms crossed over her chest, she stepped into the center. Eyes closed, she lifted her face, caught the light, and brought down the moon. Silver rays danced, and surrounded her in shimmering radiance. She twirled in their magic. Around and around.

Once.

Twice.

Three times.

Captivated, Ben held his breath. His head told him it was Bethany Ann who stood before him, but his eyes called him a liar.

In the circle a black-robed figure stood tall and slender. Brazen, confident she took in a full breath, and blew it out to the four corners.

North. South. East. West.

Wind stirred dust.

Lightning threatened rain.

Unruly raven curls whipped about her face. Above her high cheekbones, four stars tattooed in a delicate pattern added to the mystery and danger that radiated from every fiber of her being. The crescent moon glowed yellow in deep violet eyes. Ben shivered.

But it wasn't her untamed witchy beauty that made Ben's heart slam against his chest. Nope. It was her bold fearlessness that made him itch to stand by her side, march into hell, and spit right in Beelzebub's eye. Her will. Her righteousness. Her faith. Her unyielding belief in an ordained, divine purpose so powerful she dared Satan himself to challenge it. A warrior's courage. A demon fighter's defiance so fierce, men kneeled before it.

He swallowed hard. Yet again, she had transformed right before his eyes. But this time not as a crow or jaguar.

This time Bethany Ann had given way to the Daughter of the Howling Moon.

She opened her eyes to the night sky, raised an arm, and made a circular motion with her hand. Dingy-gray clouds swirled. Faster. Faster. Melted into one, becoming a churning, roaring whirlpool. A twister.

Trees struggled to cling to the earth. Thunder

boomed. He cringed. Bethany Ann stood rock solid in the circle, curled her raised hand into a fist and hit the palm of her other hand, quick and fast. Even above the howl of the whirlwind, Ben heard the hard smack.

Hail the size of walnuts pelted the church. Hail? In the Louisiana swamps? He looked at Buford. White-faced, the sheriff sank to his knees.

Once more, she pointed a finger and traced a jagged line on nature's blackboard. A lightning bolt sawed the sky in half. The hairs on Ben's arms stood at attention. The nauseating stench of sulfur tickled his nose. His stomach yawed and pitched. This was too much like battle. When arterially fire came so fast and furious, night turned to day and the bitter taste of gunpowder coated dry lips.

Everything stilled.

No roar of wind, crack of lightning or boom of thunder. Breath short and choppy, Ben marveled at nature's power. Deep-rooted trees bent. The ground shook. Rain mixed with sulfur. Deafening silence. Good God, what next? The four horsemen of the Apocalypse?

Silhouetted against the purple and red of the moon Bethany Ann stood like a fierce dark angel. If she'd drawn a flaming sword and sprouted wings, it wouldn't have surprised him one bit. He heard her voice, low and commanding.

"By the breath of Jehovah, burn this house of sin and torment to ash."

A quick snap of fingers. Sparks flew from her fingertips. Lightning zigzagged and hit the church steeple.

The church exploded into flames.

Folks poured from the building like ants from a

stomped on hill. Shouts and cries shattered the eerie quiet. One look at Bethany Ann standing dark and foreboding before them caused fear to run rampant. Men gathered their women to their sides. Children screamed, clutched their mama's skirts. Others hit their knees, called out to Jesus.

She blew out another deep breath. Wood and plaster surrendered to the white-hot air and collapsed in a smoky groaning heap.

Christ, the whole thing reminded him of a scene straight out of some nightmare.

Hungry monsters of orange and yellow flames devoured and destroyed. Ominous, black smoke roiled and choked. Frightened men, women and children cried out to be saved. Air hung heavy, drenched with the scent of burnt wood, sweat, and fear. Wind beat the sap out of trees. All under the watchful eye of a menacing, blood-red moon And all under the control of one woman…The Daughter of the Howling Moon.

Ben was both terrified and awed.

Jedidiah Wayne stumbled down the burning steps, wild-eyed, oily hair plastered against his scarred face, and a venomous water moccasin in both hands. Good God. The man looked mad as a hatter. Padded room, straight-jacket certifiable, off his rocker.

In desperation the congregation called out to him. "Deliver us from evil, Brother Jed! Deliver us!"

"Behold the great deceiver of man. Murderer. Destroyer of children."

Ben's spit turned to sand after the words had come from Bethany Ann. It wasn't any tone of voice he'd ever heard before. Forceful. Dynamic. A voice of an avenging angel who had escaped the bonds of a mortal body in order to destroy evil where it stood.

She marched toward Wayne and pointed. "Judgment day be upon you, Jedidiah Wayne. I condemn thee. Cast ye down. To burn forever in a lake of fire and brimstone."

Wayne's parishioners cowered at her thundering voice.

"Slay the soothsayer!" Wayne flung the snakes. Hissing, fangs dripping venom, the serpents flew toward her face.

"Holy-lee shit." Buford whispered and crossed himself.

Ben was tempted to do the same.

At that moment, it didn't matter that neither one of them had a Catholic bone in their body.

Chapter 42

"Bethany Ann!"

The spell of silence broken, either my fading magic or his sheer determination to warn her, Ben's voice rang out loud and clear. She raised her arms. But not to protect herself. She caught the moccasins in mid-air. They locked around her wrists and forearms like black-steeled bands. Cottonmouths closed. Tongues flicking.

Damn. If she hadn't looked like a fierce demon fighter before with dark robes and sparks conjured from her fingertips, she sure as hell did now what with poisonous water snakes wrapped round both arms. Breathtaking and scary all at the same time.

She leveled her gaze on Jedidiah. "You dare seek to kill me by turning God's innocent creations into tools of death? By His mighty word alone, I have dominion over every 'creeping thing that creepeth upon this earth.' None of His creatures will harm me. Can you say the same?"

Ben couldn't help but grin. How very clever of her. There could be no doubt in anyone's mind now that Wayne had tried to kill her. Everything that happened from this moment on would be classified as self-defense. He sighed in relief. Never should've doubted her. Smart girl, Bethany Ann.

Scrambling to keep the upper hand, Wayne turned to his worshippers. Screams and cries hushed. They gazed upon their leader with reference and certainty in their eyes. Surely evil would kneel before the great Reverend Jedidiah Wayne. After all, wasn't he God'schosen one?

He raised his hands to heaven. "Brothers. Sisters. Fear not this woman…this sorceress. For the power of the Lord is within me. I will protect you."

"Only you need to fear me this night, Jedidiah Wayne. I be no witch. But instead a warrior of God brought down from heaven to throw your soul back to hell from wince it came."

The congregation stirred and murmured.

A tough voice came from the back of the group. "If'in she cavorts with the devil, Brother Jed, why didn't them cotton moccasins strike her dead?"

Ben couldn't believe it. Someone actually had the nerve to question. A woman, brittle and hard as the voice that had come from her, pushed to the front of the milling crowd.

"She's bewitched them, Sister. Charmed them to her will."

Ben had to admit Wayne was one cool customer. But the feisty little woman wasn't buying any of it.

"Same claim can be made for you. Them serpents try to bite your hand, hiss at your touch yet bow down silent to hers. How be that?"

His followers grumbled. She had a good point.

Buford heaved his wide butt up and stood by his shoulder. "Well, now, ain't that mighty interestin'. Sounds like Bethany Ann's got an ally."

The raspy-voiced woman walked up to Bethany Ann. Looked her up and down with narrow eyes sharp as tacks. "You be Brother Jed's own daughter. He said them voodoo folks stole you away."

"No one took me. I ran and hid in the swamps." Again she pointed at the preacher. "To escape being violated by this man who dare claims to be my father. From this night forward let be it known that not one drop of Jedidiah Wayne's blood flows in my veins."

"Whoo-ee, the shit's fixin' to hit the fan now," Buford whispered.

In stunned silence, the snap, crackle, and sizzle of the fire that gnawed the church's bones sent chill bumps up Ben's arms. The congregation's murmurs fell to low whispers. He searched the crowd. Doubt and confusion crawled across their faces.

"Lying she-devil!" Wayne shouted. "Honor thy father and thy mother."

"Do not throw God's commandments against me, Jedidiah Wayne!" Bethany Ann shouted back. "Unlike you, the Spirit of the Word lives inside me, and I speak true."

Wayne pleaded to his flock. "She lies. To deceive. To cast doubt among you that the Lord God Almighty has chosen me as His one true disciple in Christ."

"For what reason would she do that?"

Ben recognized the man who asked that all-important question. John Wesley. Hanna's uncle.

Bethany Ann didn't wait for Wayne to answer.

"Because I know the truth about your daughters and am not feared to speak it."

"What?" A whip-thin woman dressed in drab gray stepped toward her. "What truth?" She glanced back at a man Ben also knew, Harvey Wilkes. "My man said our Rebecca Sue drowned accidentally. Is that what happened or not?"

"No."

Her voice turned hard as hickory. "Then you best be telling us what did."

Wayne rushed to the woman, grabbed her arm. "Listen not, Sister Naomi. This enchantress bears false witness."

All six-foot-two, two hundred pounds of Harvey Wilkes moved to his wife's side. Wayne dropped his hold. The big vein in the preacher's neck throbbed and a wild, crazed look came into his eyes. All hell was fixing to break loose. Last thing Ben wanted to do was shoot someone, but he reached for the butt of his .357 just in case. Buford stalled his hand.

"Back off, son," the sheriff said. "This here pissing match is between something far more bigger and powerful than us."

Wayne had the look of a rat caught in a trap. Panic-stricken, he rushed from one member to another. "Believe her not." The words, repeated over and over, weakened with each desperate attempt to persuade.

"Why do you fear her so?" Raspy-voice called out again. "'The truth shall set ye free.'"

Naomi Wilkes yelled out. "Let her speak."

The congregation fell silent.

Bethany Ann stepped forward.

Wayne shrank back.

The whole swamp held its breath.

"Naomi. Becky Sue fell victim to the lies and wickedness of the very man you trust to be a man of God."

Ben marveled at the compassion in Bethany Ann's voice. Her gentle tone carried as much force as her commanding one.

"I speak true." She lifted her gaze, took in every face. "Jedidiah Wayne has deceived all of you. He violates little girls, tears their innocence from them, then kills to cover up his treachery and sinful ways."

Every gaze turned to Wayne.

"Brothers. Sisters. Believe her not. I beg you."

An evil smirk crossed the preacher man's face.

"Stand steadfast," Wayne shouted. "The devil sent his witch to tempt, to make you question your faith."

Desperate move. But effective. None of his followers wanted to think they'd been duped.

"Amen! Amen!" the congregation cried out. "Go back to hell, demon!" They picked up stones. Threw them at Bethany Ann.

Ben took a step. Damned if he let them hurt her. Again Buford reached out and stopped him. "Where's your faith, boy?"

Bethany Ann's hand shot up before her, palm up. The rocks fell to the ground with not one hitting her.

"I come not from hell," she said. "I seek not to tempt, trick, or test but to speak for the dead, to avenge their deaths, and inflict justice upon their tormentor."

"She lies!" Wayne screamed, practically jumping up and down in a little-boy tantrum.

Raspy voice spoke again. "If she lies, then why does God's heavenly light shimmer and surround her while you stand in darkness?"

It was true. She stood cloaked in silver radiance. The rock-throwing and chanting stopped. Another woman spoke out.

"I be Abigail Wesley. My Hanna were sweetness itself and gentle as the songbirds she so loved. I been holding a secret for a while now. I seen Preacher grope her tiny body under the water that day at the river."

Men's heads jerked up. Shocked gasps came from the group.

"But I did nothing," Abigail continued. "Thought for sure I'd seen wrong. Nobody said nothin' to the contrary, not even Hanna. Now I hear he violated, spoiled, and kilt my little girl?"

She looked hard at Bethany Ann. "Your mama be the most god-fearing, compassionate woman I ever knowed. You swear? You swear on her sainted bones that what you say tonight be true?"

"I do."

"That be good enough for me."

"Well it ain't for me." Naomi Wilkes said. "Before I condemn a man of the cloth of such horrible, sinful things, I need to know without a shadow of doubt he did it. I ain't sure who to believe. Who be good and who be bad."

Ben groaned and glanced at Buford. There was no such proof.

"Naomi." Again the soft care in Bethany Ann's voice touched Ben. "If you heard the words from your own daughter's lips, then would you believe?"

"Necromancer!" Wayne shouted. "I say again, Brothers and Sisters, she is of the devil. Believe her not!"

The crowd grew restless again. The sour scent of sweat and fear drenched the air.

Wouldn't take much to blow the lid right of this powder keg of emotions.

"Hold thy tongue, blasphemer! Did not Peter raise Tabitha? Paul breathe life back into Eutcyshus? Both Elijah and Elisha called the soul back as well. Jesus laughed in the face of Death. Dare you call them necromancers? Demonic?"

Ben grinned. *Sic em, Bethany Ann.*

She returned her gaze to Naomi. "I ask again. If you hear the truth from your daughter's own mouth, do you swear to believe?"

Naomi left the group. Walked up within a foot before Bethany Ann. Her voice trembled yet came determined.

"Last time I seen my Becky Sue we had words over something stupid. I told her to git out of my sight. That be the day she died. Tore my innards to shreds. I cry every night and beg God to give me a second chance so I could tell my little girl how much I loved her."

She took a deep breath.

"If'in you can bring my baby girl back even for a split hair, I'll not only believe but get down on knees and praise Jesus. And for the rest of my days, I'd tell God how grateful I am that he sent his angel to make it so."

The men said nothing, just shook their heads in agreement. But it was a different story with the women…the mothers. They gathered around Naomi. Joined hands. Bowed their heads. Whispered amens.

Wayne stood flat-foot and white-faced. Ben nudged the sheriff. They eased up in the shadows behind the preacher ready to give chase if he decided to bolt and run.

Bethany Ann heaved a deep sigh.

"Then. So be it."

Chapter 43

Ben gritted his teeth. *Don't do it, Bethany Ann. Don't do it.* He'd seen those girls after being under the water. Patches of skin chewed raw. Black, wormy eyes. No mother should see their babies broken and empty.

"This isn't good, Buford. She shouldn't do this."

"I'm surprised at you, boy. That gal has right on her side. She ain't gonna do nothing wrong."

She stepped back into the circle, took a deep breath, and shut her eyes.

The night closed in around them. Dark. Still. So quiet he could hear hearts beating. Thump-thump, fast, Thump slow. Thump, thump fast again.

The radiance around her began to swirl. Like a carousel at the county fair, the light spun slow gaining speed with every turn.

Silver light against black night.

Dark hair streaked with opalescent moonbeams.

Beautiful. Mesmerizing.

Solemn, reverent, she stood in a whirling funnel of snowy light. Careful, as if handling finely spun glass, she collected the brightness one strand at a time until a glowing ball rested in her palms.

She stretched forth her hands.

"Semblez."

He glanced at Buford.

"French word. Means appear, the sheriff explained.

The glimmering orb floated from her hand leaving a kite tale of twinkling sparks trailing behind.

Everyone gasped at the same time.

The illuminated sphere hesitated before the tree line then melted into a cascade of pearly light.

Rebecca Sue Wilkes stepped out of the dissolved radiance.

"Good Gawd Almighty," Buford whispered.

"You said a mouthful," Ben replied.

Chapter 44

"Mommy?"

"Oh, my God," Naomi cried. "Becky? Baby is that you?"

"Where are you, Mommy?"

"I'm here, baby girl. Right here."

Their cries threw Ben back into memory to a hot, dry summer when he and Danni had found a dead fawn. Its mama bleated mournfully for a baby that would never return. Such a gut-wrenching sound. Danni had collapsed in tears. Becky Sue's small pitiful voice, just like that doe's bruised his heart. How could a mother survive this?

"Come here, Becky. Come to mama."

"No."

"Oh, honey. Don't be feared. I'm sorry I yelled at ya that day. Mama didn't mean it." Sobs choked her words. "Please, baby. Just come to mama."

"Not as long as he's there."

"Who? Becky Sue. Who?"

"Preacher."

"Why?"

Unaware he'd been holding his breath, Ben's lungs about burst. He gasped in air. The moment of truth was at hand.

"He hurt me. Slapped me and threw me down. Ripped off my pretty blue dress."

Shit. He couldn't stand it.

He shot a look at Bethany Ann. She stood ramrod straight, eyes squeezed shut. The tears streaming down her cheeks betrayed her hard stillness. No longer caring if he gave up his position, he ran to her.

"For the love of God, Bethany Ann. Stop this. They don't need to hear."

She turned to him. The crescent moon in her eyes, only a faint sliver floating in their dampness.

"Yes they do, Benjamin. There can be no doubt."

Shit.

"It ain't easy for me neither, Benjamin. Her soul be tied to mine in this light. I feel the hurt. The pain of each pinch. Every slap. Each bite. Smell his rancid breath. Feel his rough lips. Calloused hands pawing, fondling. His hardness defiling, ripping away innocence and purity. Feel her confusion. Her betrayal. Her helplessness."

Shit.

Becky Sue's cries made him shiver.

"He kissed my hair. Laid on top of me." Tears strangled her. "It hurt bad, Mommy."

Naomi crumbled to her knees. Abigail kneeled, put an arm around the woman's shoulders, no doubt hurting just as bad knowing her own Hanna had suffered the same horrible fate.

"He held me under the water. Wouldn't let me up. It was dark and cold. No air. I was scairt real bad. But then I saw Hanna, and I weren't 'fraid no more."

Abigail lifted her gaze. "You saw my Hanna?"

"Yes'um. Her and Sarah Rose."

He felt Bethany Ann tense.

"Sarah Rose told us to be brave cause a beautiful

angel with dark hair and pretty purple eyes would come and set us free. Then all of us would go to heaven. Don't cry no more, Mommy. Sarah Rose is taking good care of me and Hanna now. But, I sure do hope that angel comes soon 'cause I'm really tired of waiting.

Shit.

Only a man with a rock heart and frosted blood could handle this. The sting of tears made him look away. Stare vacant into the dying embers of the burning church. Mankind. What a cruel breed. Bullies always pounding on the innocent, destroying, killing. If God is love and man created in his image, then why? Bethany Ann claimed most folks were good. But it only takes one bad apple to spoil the whole barrel. Right? Even she had been worn down by the never-ending struggle.

God, he was such a hypocrite. Violence made him sick yet his job was just that. It took all he had not to put a bullet right between Wayne's eyes. The weasely, self-absorbed prick. One shot would end his arrogant smirk. His cruelty. He murdered Mom. Caused Danni to end her life. Oh how he wanted to kill the son-of-a-bitch. Not only kill, but torture. Make him suffer. Cut his balls off. Scream for mercy.

Just like those little girls had.

Becky Sue's voice made him turn back.

"Don't you fret none, Mommy. I'm going to see Jesus."

And just like that, Rebecca Sue Wilkes was gone.

Wayne's sneer made Ben shake with anger. "Sister Naomi. The witch has you locked in her spell. That be not your daughter, but a phantom conjured to trick you. Turn you against me. Against God."

"No!" Naomi crawled to her feet. Stood tall and

downright mean looking. Mama bear mean.

"It be you who deceives. You think a mama don't know her own child? 'Sides that blue dress you stripped off my girl's tiny body be what we argued about that day." She gazed at the faces around her. "The dress was new. Sewed it by lantern light after Becky went to bed at night. It were a surprise. Took weeks to make. She wanted to play in it that awful day. I forbid her." Her gaze returned to the preacher. "No witch. No demon. No trickster would know that."

Only the crackling of the dying fire could be heard.

Everyone turned to the preacher. "Explain that," the unspoken question in every eye.

Wayne searched the faces of his followers. Licked his lips.

Get out of this one, you slippery bastard.

In a sudden move, Wayne dropped to his knees, and folded his hands in prayer.

"Oh Lord God Almighty. I pray thee. Help them understand. I loved those beautiful young lambs. Loved their snowy skin. Their heavenly green eyes. Loved the smell, the touch of their golden silky hair."

What kind of prayer was that? Ben wanted to kick him.

"Help them see I had to save them. Fill them full of the Holy Spirit. Course they resisted my righteousness. Hollered and fought. That's what the devil does when touched by the Holy Ghost."

"Enough!"

Harvey Wilkes charged from the crowd. Yanked the preacher up by the collar. Shook him like a rat. "You lying no good bastard. You kilt her. My little girl. Raped and killed."

"No! No!" Wayne screamed. "I never wanted to kill. I loved those young'uns. It ain't my fault. Just like Adam in the Garden of Eden. The woman tempted me."

What the hell was he talking about?"

"Enough of your jibber-jabber, Preacher. Speak plain 'fore I rip your head off."

"Hester. Hester made me drown them. Said no mortal man would want them, care for them after being with the Son of God. They'd wander all alone. I had to send them back to the Father for their own good."

Hester! Damn. In all the excitement Ben hadn't given one thought to the bitch. Where was she anyway? Harvey's loud roar shook the ground.

"There be only one Son of God. And you ain't him."

A fist big as a bear paw smacked Wayne full in the face.

The preacher hit the ground. Blood gushed from a broken nose.

Harvey went for him again. "I'm gonna break every bone in your body, you son-of-a bitch."

"Benjamin."

Bethany Ann's still, small voice surprised him.

"Stop him. Let the only bloodshed tonight be on my hands."

Out of the corner of his eye, Ben saw the sheriff grab Harvey and pull him off the preacher.

Wayne scrambled to his feet. Ran into the swamp.

He rushed to help Buford pin Harvey's arms behind his back.

"Harvey. Harvey listen to me," Ben pleaded.

"He's gettin' away," Harvey yelled. "The bastard is gettin' away."

"No. I promise you. We'll catch him. Let the law

handle this."

Just as fast as his rage had consumed him, it left the big man in one big whoosh. Buford loosened his hold.

"You don't understand. She was my baby." Shoulders large enough to carry the world but not strong enough to bear his pain, slumped. His tortured sob sent a knife through Ben's heart. "Got three boys. But Becky Sue was my only girl. I should've known. Should've stopped him. He *hurt* her. Took her from me. And…and I couldn't save her."

He'd seen grown men weep in the war. The sight liked to have destroyed him. The tears running down Harvey Wilkes's face damn threw him over the edge. Took all he had not to shy away.

"Harvey, I swear to you. Jedidiah Wayne won't get away with it. He'll answer for everything he's done."

"How can you be so sure of that, deputy?"

"Because good always destroys evil."

Harvey cocked an eyebrow. "You're a deputy sheriff. Heard tell an ex-soldier too. No doubt you've seen a passel of bad in your life. Do you honest to God believe what you just said?"

He glanced over at Bethany Ann.

"I do. I believe."

Harvey followed his glance. "I ain't rightly sure what all went on here tonight. Don't know what that gal standing over there be." A shake of his head.

"She's an angel sent down from heaven, that's what she be," Naomi spoke up. "An angel sent from God to answer my prayer. Gave me a second chance. Nothin' else matters."

He shrugged loose from the sheriff. Walked over to Bethany Ann.

"You make him pay."

Harvey's glance swept the congregation, then returned to stare straight into her eyes.

"Do whatever needs to be done. You have my word no one here will raise a finger again' ya.

"Not today.

Not tomorrow.

Not ever."

Chapter 45

I ain't never seen snow. Truth be, the only time I recall it got bad cold was that day I dropped my Big Chief tablet at Granny LeBeaux's pond. I seen a photo once in Life Magazine of a snowy Christmas Eve up north somewhere. It were so pretty, I cut it out and pasted it on my bedroom wall.

On those hot, muggy, Louisiana summer nights when nothing crawls but sweat-drenched stink down your neck, I'd stare at the picture, and pretend I stood in the middle of that cold. I'd shiver in air so sharp it hurt to draw breath. Reach out to touch an ice-crystal moon surrounded by diamond-pointed stars. Their reflection thrown across the mountain stream below, a blanket of glazed white so brilliant, I'd squint in the brightness. Everything so still I could hear owl wings in the dark. Smell the damp. See the frosted breath of every critter what moved.

I stood in the circle and called that scene to me. When I opened my eyes, the fire of the Howling Moon had cooled to the icy white of a Christmas Moon. The blood from Jedidiah's side-ways nose, a crimson path before me. Not that a trail was necessary.

As a jaguar, all I needed was the mystery of deep night to find my prey.

Benjamin stood by the sheriff, wide-eyed and a little peaked lookin.' Bless his heart. Hearing him say he believed damn near busted my heart wide open.

At long last, his soul had found its way home.

Harvey Wilkes yelled out again. "Wayne's probably halfway to Tuscaloosa by now. How you gonna find him in the dark?"

Ben's gaze locked with mine.

I glanced at the congregation. Every eye trained on me. They'd witnessed enough this night. Besides they were on my side. Weren't no need to spook them any more than what I already had and spoil it all. Ben heard my thoughts. He turned to Harvey.

"You let me and the sheriff worry about that. Best thing all of you can do now is go home and let us do our job."

Feisty woman called from the crowd. "What about Hester? She's in this just as deep as the preacher. What'ya gonna do about her?"

Angry rumbles stirred the air again. The sheriff stepped forward.

"Deputy Sol will go after Wayne. I'll find Hester. The rest of yas go on home." More grumbles. Buford raised his hands.

"Folks, y'all know me. Know my word is gold. I promise each and every one of yas justice will be done. It's late. Your young'uns need to be in bed. Go on home, now."

"We'll hold you to that, Sheriff Tate," John Wesley yelled out.

Still grumbling, the crowd splintered off and disappeared.

The sheriff touched Ben's sleeve. I heard him whisper.

"Ben, traipsing through the dark in a swamp plumb

full of all sorts of creepy crawlies hunting a fella as crazy as Wayne is a young man's game. I'm going after Hester. I know what Bethany Ann can do. Just the same, you watch your back out there." He glanced my way. "And hers too. She may be powerful, but she's still flesh and blood. You hear me?"

Ben nodded. "Yes, sir. Hester's just as crafty. Be careful."

"Always am."

"Buford? You know Bethany Ann won't let me bring Wayne back alive, don't ya?"

"Son, after what I seen and heard here tonight what makes you think I give a damn?"

Buford stomped to his car and gunned the engine. The headlights from the Ford bobbed between the trees like ghostly lanterns.

Benjamin waited for me by the tree line.

I walked to the nearest cypress. Draped in bolts of Spanish moss, the tree stood young and tall. I knelt at his feet, placed one hand on the moist dirt and the other against his smooth bark. Eyes closed, I whispered.

"Roots below arise this night. Seek. Find. And bind tight."

The earth rumbled and shook. Ripping. Tearing. Long roots broke from the dirt. Crawled like gnarled daddy-long-leg spiders into the swamp. Benjamin jumped out of their way and swore.

"Always knew those damn trees were human."

Chapter 46

Ben didn't want to lose sight of the black cat. But to no avail. She moved too fast. A blur. Just a hint of black smoke in the misty air.

No need to move quiet, like that was even possible in this crispy-green, overgrown fungus pit. Those damn tree roots gave him the heebie-jeebies. They thrashed and groaned. Had a mind of their own. Spooky. Like wooden tentacles crawling through the undergrowth.

A scream threw his heart into overdrive.

Pistol drawn, Ben rounded the corner. The sight before him punched his gut, robbed him of air.

Jedidiah Wayne hung suspended between two trees. Arms stretched out on either side, held tight by roots that had climbed up the bark and snared him. Feet tied together, bound taut. Reminded him so much of those pictures in Sunday school of Jesus nailed to the cross that he shook his head at the irony. Suppose it was only fitting.

The jaguar crouched a few feet from the preacher's dangling body ready to spring.

"Shoot her! Shoot her!" Wayne hollered.

She'll toy with him first then maul him to shreds. Wasn't sure if he should stop her or not.

"Bennie."

"Danni?"

She appeared from the mist. Golden hair almost

222

white in the moon's glow. Again breath escaped him.

"Leave it be. 'For whatsoever a man soweth, that shall he also reap.' "

Ben holstered his .357.

The jaguar leaped. Caught Wayne around his waist. Sunk claws deep through skin straight into bone.

Agonized shrieks stirred the bile in Ben's gut.

She raked razor claws down both legs. Tender flesh ripped and tore, fell in bloody strips to the dirt.

Muscles taut, she jumped again. This time wicked claws sliced his back. The cat and the preacher twirled in the air in a macabre, slow-moving dance.

The branches broke.

Preacher and cat hit the ground at the same time.

Wayne grabbed the broken branch. Swung it hard at the jaguar. How did he even have the strength to twitch after the pain she'd inflicted on him?

He not only heard but felt the sickening thud of wood hitting her.

She rolled ass-over-teakettle into the brush.

Bethany Ann!

Pissed as hell, the cat flung an angry roar into the night. Made Ben jump back. Bite his lip.

She was finished playing.

Ears pinned flat. Fangs barred. Low and sleek, black death stalked, one step after another toward the preacher squirming on the ground.

Wayne kicked at her. She caught his boot between strong jaws. Sharp teeth cut through the leather slicker than snot. The snap and crunch of breaking bone made the bile in Ben's gut shoot up his gullet.

Rip. Shake. Tear.

The sight of her gnawing on the preacher's foot

made him gag.

The copper stink of blood clogged his nose. The sour taste of vomit burned the back of his throat.

Wayne raised his arm ready to strike again with the branch. How? How could he even move?

Before the thought was even finished, he knew.

Evil never gives up. Holds tough. Dies hard.

In one fluid, easy leap the cat caught the branch in midair. The sound of popping gristle, an arm ripped from its socket, torn from its body, sent Ben into another gagging fit. War had been hell. But this was animal savagery. Pure belly-rolling butchery.

Tearing pieces of skin from his chest, she continued her savage attack.

An ear here. A finger there. One pink, tender piece at a time.

Shit. She's skinning him alive. Half-alive anyway.

Snap. Pop. The cat sunk her teeth in the side of Wayne's neck and shook him like a rag doll. Buckets of blood stained the ground deep red.

Holding his limp body tight in her mouth, she dragged him through the weeds. Ben staggered after her.

Where the hell was she going?

She stopped at the river's edge. Dropped the preacher cold. The sharp crack of his head bouncing off rock sent chills racing up Ben's spine. Wayne's one arm plopped heavy into the mud and muck.

She gazed into the wild. Uttered high-pitched chattering into the wind.

Air turned cool. Mist moved in. The silver light of the moon tarnished to a dull glow. He'd swear he heard whispers all around him. Trees. Bushes. Crickets. Owls. Like they were talking to one another. All of one mind, one spirit.

He gulped. He knew then. Knew her chatter had been a call. A summons to the spirit of the swamp.

Water rippled.

Oh God.

Quick. Silent. Deadly. The gator sliced through the scum and reeds.

Vicious and swift the tough-skinned killer clamped down on Jedidiah, dragged him under the water. Ben heard stories about a gator's famous death roll but never believed it. Until now. Satisfied its victim was dead, the gator shredded and tore. Gorged itself on Wayne's tender carcass.

It was only fitting.

Live by the flesh. Die by the flesh.

Chapter 47

Gasping for air, Ben turned his back on the gruesome scene. He glanced over at the black cat. Nose wrinkled, she rubbed her head and the side of her mouth in the dirt. No doubt getting rid of any taste of vile preacher that lingered on her tongue.

He slumped against a tree, slid down the cool bark to his knees. Felt like he'd run miles. His head pounded.

It was over.

Finally, it was over.

"You bitch!"

His heart slammed against his ribs. What the hell?

Hester Wayne charged from the thick growth of trees and brush. Where the hell had she come from? Not important. The meat cleaver clutched in her white-knuckled hand was.

Her screams, hysterical, inhuman, made him shake. Eyes wide, dark and vacant. Hair flying wild and tumbled. Good God, the woman had gone over the edge, never to return. Crazy as a loon.

She hissed. Spit burning words of acid at the jungle cat.

"Woman or cat makes no difference to me. I know who you are, you black witch. I'm gonna make you pay. Hack your precious deputy sheriff to pieces. Alive. Right in front of ya. Just like you did to my Jed. Then I'm coming after you. 'An eye for an eye,' saith the Lord."

The cleaver held high, she rushed toward Ben.

He struggled to his feet. Fumbled for his holster. The .357 firm in his hand, he squeezed the trigger.

The bullet hit Hester's shoulder. She dropped the blade. Stumbled. Staggered backwards into the river.

The scaly predator attacked quick as lightning.

Her shrieks were lost as the gator grabbed her leg, dragged her underneath the muddy, churning water.

Pinned her. Drowned her.

Children's voices cut the air.

Heart racing, he turned. For the hundredth time that day, the air left this body.

Hanna, Becky Sue, and Sarah Rose stood by the bank.

"Now she knows firsthand how it feels to die. Alone. In the cold and dark," Becky Sue said.

"What goes around comes around," Sarah Rose answered.

"It's only fittin'," Hanna replied.

Chapter 48

Benjamin and me never talked about that night.

I'd stayed away from him on purpose. Figured he needed time to get a hold on everything what happened. But about two months after the church burning, I caught his thoughts.

I took to wing and sky.

If'in anyone would've told me I'd be sitting on Granny LeBeaux's back porch steps, I'd of called them a liar. Somewhere Sarah Rose be laughing her butt off. Yet, here I be. Sitting alongside Benjamin. Chewing the fat. Sharing bottles of Grape Nehi in the shank of the evening.

He'd fixed up the old homestead right nice. Cut down the weeds, gave the house a new coat of paint. Dreamboat Blue. Like his eyes. Even painted the barn a bright red. Funny how all barns be colored red. Don't know why. Just one of them mysteries of life I reckon.

"Granny likes what you done to the place," I said. "And that you live here now."

"Really? You know that for a fact?"

Couldn't help but grin at the tease in his voice. "Yes. She done told me so."

His eyebrow cocked, and that old familiar look of disbelief crawled across his face.

Guess he'd always question. Couldn't help it. Just the way God made him. It be all good. To my way of thinking, the world needed men like Benjamin who doubted and wondered. Kept folks on their toes.

"She talks to me a lot. She was at the church that…that night."

He about dropped his soda.

"You mean that feisty, rough-voiced woman was Granny LeBeaux?"

"Oh, Benjamin for a lawman at times you ain't very ____"

"Savvy. Yeah, so you've said." He laughed.

He was different. More relaxed. Didn't pace no more. Told me earlier that evening, his belly quit hurting too. His face had that smooth look of someone who slept at night and dreamed good things, not tormented by ghosts of past memories and regrets.

Benjamin was a man at peace.

"Well, I'm glad I have her blessing," he said. "For some reason, I liked the place the first time I saw it. Didn't seem right to watch it go to ruin. Got more fixing up to do. Need a new stove in the kitchen. Refrigerator, too." He winked. "Grape Nehi tastes better cold, ya know."

He finished his drink with a loud burp. I giggled. He ducked his head. Not because he was embarrassed. Benjamin always lowered his head and studied his boots when something was on his mind. All I had to do was wait. When he was ready, he'd tell me.

It were a nice evening. A warm breeze tickled my face bringing with it the sweet, fresh smell of honeysuckle that I couldn't get enough of. Daylight melted into dusk. Stars popped out.

One minute they weren't there, then bang, there they be. I never got tired of seeing that miracle.

It was that magic time of day when all things mysterious came out of shadow to play.

"Bethany Ann? The girls? Are they with Jesus now?"

"Yes."

"Without a doubt?"

"Yes."

"Good."

He cleared his throat.

" I've been doing some thinking. This house is big enough for two. Why not move in? You don't need to worry what folks say. After all this ruckus, you can do no wrong. Besides, Naomi Wilkes would shoot anyone who dared talk bad about ya."

"Both Naomi and Abigail have taken quite a liken' to me, that's for sure. But I ain't the only one." I glanced over at him. "They think you hung the moon."

"Buford Tate's retiring. Said this case made an old man out of him. He wants me to run for sheriff."

"Are ya?"

"Yeah, think I'll try my hand at it. For a while anyway. I might need some help, though."

"Me?"

"Sure. Why not? There's always going to be innocents in need of protection and justice. And we make a good team. Besides, if Buford can have a Voodoo Priestess as his confidant and informant, why can't I have a shape-shifting Warrior of God as mine?"

I laughed.

"Which brings me back to my offer. Move in here. I can't have my partner living in the boonies. You know how much I hate that damn swamp."

I shook my head and watched a couple of gray feral

cats drink milk I'd put out for them. It were the least I could do, what with them probably being Sissy Cat's kin and all.

"You know how I feel about the swamp, Benjamin. The wild calls me. Pulls me to its core. Settles my innards. Gives me peace."

"I got an inside bathroom with a tub and shower."

Damn. He wasn't playing fair. "Mighty temptin', I'll give ya that."

"Well, look. If you don't want to move into the house, how about the barn? I could fix it up. If you can live in a broken down two-room shack, why not a barn?"

"Well…maybe. But what's your wife gonna say when she finds out?"

"What!?"

The look on his face threw me into a fit of giggles. Oh how I loved to shock him.

"Bethany Ann. Damnit. Quit laughing. This is serious. My wife? You have a vision? Who is she? Quit laughing!"

I put down the empty pop bottle and stepped off the porch.

"Good night, Benjamin."

"You gonna tell me or not?"

I just grinned.

Chapter 49

"Well, now. Ain't *that* mighty interesting."

Buford Tate reared back in his chair, a possum grin on his face.

"She really said you're gonna get hitched?"

Ben chuckled. "What? You think that's so impossible?"

"Nope. Not at all. Every filly in this here Parish be after you. Bethany Ann give ya any clues on who this woman is?"

"Nope. Not one.

"Maybe it's her."

"Buford. Give it up. I'm too old for her. Besides we never had that kind of relationship."

"Son, that gal beats the socks off of any woman walking. She saved the children. Gave you back your faith. Not to mention, she's the prettiest girl I ever laid eyes on. Why if I were thirty years younger, I'd be after her in a heartbeat. Better scoop her up before some young buck beats ya to it."

"Doubt that will ever happen."

"What makes you so sure?"

Ben leaned back in his chair, plopped his boots up on the desk.

"Because Bethany Ann is a daughter of The Howling Moon."

He smiled.

"And she bows before no man."

A word about the author...

R.H. Burkett is a public speaker, an international, professional Tarot card reader, contest judge, an award winning author with short stories in several anthologies, a list of contest wins, and four published books. She's served on the Board of Directors for the Ozark Writers League and was the former paranormal editor and advertising manager for Oghma Creative Media.

She resides in Springdale, Arkansas. rhburkett.com

Thank you for purchasing
this publication of The Wild Rose Press, Inc.

For questions or more information
contact us at
info@thewildrosepress.com.

The Wild Rose Press, Inc.
www.thewildrosepress.com